The Excluded

Fire Child

J.D. Hines

Acknowledgements:

I want to thank all the readers of my books, who got the series *this* far. All the way to Conrad's book, the fire child, himself. Thank you so much for staying with my books, and I hope you stick around for Timothy's story!

Chapter One: To Refuse

A black beetle with orange spots going along his wings scuttled across the cement, stopping when it reached Conrad's boot, slim antennas feeling the structure it stumbled upon. Conrad contemplated crushing it under the sole of his boot, then discarded the thought as soon as it entered his head. If one thing was for certain, he drew no resemblance to Gary Swift, who would have squashed the bug in a heartbeat, smearing its' insides along the cement with his converse sneaker.

He allowed the beetle to climb on to the top of his boot, getting situated in the laces, exploring its new environment. It had two seconds…Oh, well. Conrad violently shook his foot, startling the beetle, who braced its wings then took off into the air, free from all complication's life hurled its way, soaring through the sky, on its way to-whatever. He didn't care. Conrad shook his hands, stretching his arms out in front of himself. He then preceded to roll his head around his shoulder blades, only satisfied when he heard a small crack. He then shoved a hand into his pocket, moving it around until he heard the clank of car keys. He then glanced over his shoulder at his grandmother's squat, one story house, nothing but silence by the front door area.

Liz had already limped inside her room to take a nap, which usually lasted for more than a few hours, giving him more than enough time to make it to Refuse, his future home with the other pyoglees of Cove City, and about a few miles away, the land of the Canids, the place Conrad would rather be a million miles away from, breathing in fresh air and not the stench of those mutts who formed in packs, or big groups of people.

Needing others to constantly come to their rescue instead of han-
dling the problem themselves disgusted Conrad, always grateful he'd
been born a Pyroglee, learning how to look out for himself instead of
depending on others.

He jammed the key into the lock then jerked the door open when he
felt sure he'd be able to climb inside. Along with backing out of the
driveway, he twisted the dial next to the steering wheel, searching for
his favorite country station, the one his mother used to listen to whenever she wanted to sit back and relax, drowning out the memories of
her old life. His father used to become annoyed whenever he heard
the tunes coming out of their old radio, sometimes changing the station to classic rock songs, complaining he didn't want to listen to
some sad, old folks who always messed up his eardrums simply by
opening their fat mouths.

Conrad snickered and turned the sound up then swerved the car
onto a highway, foot pressed onto the gas pedal, hoping he wouldn't
pass any patrol cars on the lookout for any vehicle driving above the
speed limit. Well, Conrad didn't dare drive faster than what the law
told them to abide by, but he still didn't want to get pulled over by

some over-eager cop who couldn't wait to hand out a ticket.

The exit to Refuse showed itself in the distance on a white board with the letters painted a dark grey, almost black, giving the appearance he was about to enter a haunted land with red eyed scarecrows who had mangy fur, holding worms they plucked from the dirt in their beaks. He may not have been greeted by bone thin scarecrows or phantoms with their arms outstretched and fingers clinched, but his nerves began to run amok inside him as he began to remember the point of him even going to Refuse in the first place.

A few days ago, he'd gotten a call on his cell phone, some of the silver paint having had peeled off the surface, a mousy voice who he had recognized as Lauren Janeal, a girl who was also fifteen, urged him to make his way back to their town as quickly as he could. She wouldn't go into detail about any of the events which were about to transpire, but he could tell they weren't good. And her forced hang up let him know higher up townsmen had gotten close by.

He had heard that same summer the townspeople were required to take part in some type of weird, coming together ceremony, or some crap like that. And for some reason, they thought it would be pivotal for him to make an appearance.

"Pfft." Conrad turned the wheel to the right, exiting the highway, then drove down the street until he spotted the dirt road, a dirt road headed straight to the back part of Refuse, where all the pyroglees made their residence. Well, most of the pyroglees. Conrad knew he was going to be forced to live in the same place as soon as he graduated from Warren's Refuge of Neglected Gifted, with the rest of the pyroglees at his school.

He sped down the road, noticing the squat houses, tiled roofs with paint peeled off of them, front doors chipped and some of them burned on the edges or full on in the center as if someone went on a flame throwing spree. Conrad sighed and noticed the downtown area of the town straight ahead, where a group of people gathered around in black slacks and worn out hats with long flaps which waved up and down in the wind.

He immediately stomped on the break once he pulled up next to a wooden bench, nearly running into the structure, causing splintered wood to fling into the air and hit the sides of the car.

A couple of the people startled, wheeling around to face whoever had nearly plowed into their property. Conrad shut the engine off then scooted to the passenger seat since he couldn't possibly get out on the driver's side, not with part of the bench blocking the way.

"Conrad!" One of the men waved as he hopped out of the car, slamming the door shut afterwards. *Mayor Davidson.* Conrad spit on the ground next to his foot, images of the man on tv screens inside shops gloating about the high quality of their town popping into his head. *What now?*

Mayor Davidson slowly walked toward Conrad, accompanied by guards on either side of him, their eyes shielded by the tips of their hats, some with their hands on top of their pockets, pistols shielded from Conrad's sight. Oh, but he knew they were there, along with cans of pepper spray they kept in their other pockets.

"Right on time," said Davidson, hands placed on his waists when he got closer to the boy, about more than several feet away. "You have been chosen to complete a little exercise we're putting on for the next several days." Conrad shook his head, unbelief at what he heard spilling inside his mind like murky water.

"I didn't agree to do this," he snapped, anger now clawing at him, telling him to go back to Liz as quickly as he possibly could. "Find somebody else-or better yet, why don't you do it? You're the mayor of this town. Put on a show for everybody."

Mayor Davidson's eyes narrowed into slits, lips bending into a frown and thin nostrils letting out a puff of air once he snorted.

"Young man," he said, voice no longer coming off as pleasant but frustrated and maybe a little angry. The guards standing next to him moved a little bit closer to him. "You have been picked simply be-cause your mother is well respected in this town and these people will follow anyone closely related to her. We need you to be an example. To not just everyone here, but further out as well."

"Further out?" Conrad crossed his arms, thinking the man in front of him must have completely lost it. They haven't even told him what they wanted him to do and yet they expected him to follow along like some idiot who never said 'no'.

"Well, yes," said Davidson with uncertainty, eyes looking behind Conrad, and he began to beckon furtively for someone to come for-ward. Conrad resisted looking over his shoulder, not wanting to take his eyes off the man in front of him, who was growing more nervous with every second passing by.

Two more guards came forward, with their shoulders so close to-gether they almost hid what stood behind them, but Conrad immedi-ately noticed leather boots in back of their legs, shiny, as if someone just scrubbed them, making sure to get all the dirt off. Eyes narrow-ing, teeth clinching, Conrad hoped for the mayor's sake, for whoever stood behind the guard's sake…heck, for his own sake, because he could already feel the heat burning his hands, that whoever stood hid-den in back of the guards wasn't who he thought he could possibly be. No. Davidson couldn't be that monstrously cruel.

"Remember," continued Davidson, a toothless smile spreading up his face. "We need you two to serve as an example to your townsmen and women. To put aside your differences as a pyroglee…" He waved for the two guards to step apart. To Conrad's utter disbelief and downright fury, came the utterly stuck-up face of someone he hated seeing at school every day, heat spreading to his fingers faster than he could ever remember. "and canid."

And who should appear soon after the guards stepped aside but none other than Maddox Bernard, himself, chewing on a half-eaten sandwich, eyes observing his surroundings, having an uncaring tint to them until they landed on Conrad.

The other boy's nails began to transform into sharp claws at the same time Conrad figured his irises had changed to a blood red color. He thought he had every right to show just how infuriated he really was, considering blowing up every shop in the town square.

If Mayor Davidson wanted to see a canid explode into a burst of searing hot flames, Conrad was more than happy to provide him with the show.

Chapter two: A Hesitant Partnership

Any sense of calmness trying to push its way into Conrad, creating

an acceptance to his current situation, was dashed into a million

pieces, the pyroglee instincts hissing at him to 'go'.

He threw away any sense of rationality residing in him and rushed

at the other boy who shouldn't even be in the same place as him, to

keep his place with the other canids. Where he belonged. Before Con-

rad and Maddox could even reach each other, someone with a firm

grip grabbed his shoulders, pulling him back so his shoes scraped against the ground. He kicked his feet, struggling to get himself out of the guard's grip, the fact that three more guards came to hold him back once they realized he was escaping from the first man only incensed him even more.

"Keep them away from each other!" came Mayer Davidson's frazzled voice, an arm wrapping around Conrad's chest paired with another man shoving him backwards. And above all things, Maddox finally stopped trying to fight his way to Conrad and stood unmoving with a smirk on his face, his teeth making an appearance.

"Let me go!" Conrad wrenched a guard's arm down from around his chest, almost throwing him to the ground, hoping he ripped the man's arm out of its' socket.

"Calm down, boy," urged Davidson. "We're only doing this for the good of our people. This whole thing is set to make everything better-"

"How?!" Conrad belted, heat no longer burning his hands but spreading up his neck and face as well. "You trick me into coming here then expect me to do whatever you say? Find somebody else to do your stupid project."

"For years, our people have been feared and looked down upon," said Mayor Davidson, slowly shaking his head. "Instead of joining together with others who are facing the same thing, we're separated, told to hate each other. But we can soon end this, my boy. By joining ranks, we now have the upper hand."

Standing still, a memory from last year of Ethan telling him the same thing flashed in his mind, how Conrad had snapped at him then stormed past the other boy, not wanting to hear another word. Maybe he should have stayed put and actually listened like a normal human being. Instead, he had let his temper get the best of him, crowding his thoughts and not letting him understand what he could possibly mean. But this…

Inviting a canid into their territory so he could prove a point, and even worse, a canid he couldn't stand to be even a few inches from.

"You never told me about any of this." Conrad shook his sleeves out in front of himself, refusing to look in Maddox's direction, knowing that if he did, he'd burst into a full-on sprint towards him again, flames shooting out of his fingertips at the arrogant boy. "Never let me know about you inviting a mongrel into our town-"

"Now, wait a minute-"

"*But*, if this is going to slow down the Swift's plan they have going

on right now, I'm willing to try. Because as much as I hate *him*," he

nodded in Maddox's direction. "I can't stand Bertram even more."

"Good," Mayor Davidson clapped his hands together, reminding

Conrad of some overachieving kid who answered a question correctly

in class and sat at his desk grinning like he'd solved a bunch of math

problems in a matter of seconds. "Bring them over to the middle of

the square. I want to get started as quickly as possible." Conrad was

once again grabbed by his shoulders, but instead of being shoved

backwards he was being pushed forward.

He briefly wondered if Maddox was being treated the same way,

but the stupid boy merely walked past him in a slow gait, tossing the

last chunk of the sandwich into his mouth then wiping his hands after-

ward by slapping them together.

As Davidson had said, they eventually came to a stop in the very

middle of the square, street lights lining the pathways in front of little

shops of clothing stores, salons, and one grocery store. They all

formed a half circle around them, except Conrad saw no one inside the establishments. In fact, the entire square was devoid of pedestrians strolling down the sidewalks, window shopping or grabbing a quick bite to eat by stopping at a food cart.

"Now," said Davidson, crossing his arms after motioning for the guards to back away. "What I want both of you to do is convince others from your districts why joining together is our best option. We can't stay away from each other if we plan to fight back."

"Hold on." Maddox raised one finger in the air, an unamused smile on his face. "You expect me to return to my town a pyroglee lover? You're out of your mind." As much as Conrad didn't want to admit it, he couldn't help but agree with the other boy, thinking their mayor lost all of his sanity, himself. "Is this some sort of joke?"

"Not at all." Mayor Davidson took on a more serious tone, brows narrowed, lips pursed. "I simply want you to work together to accomplish this goal. To show everyone that pyroglees and canids can join forces. Starting with step one: Getting you guys used to each other." Conrad jerked his head to the front so he had Maddox in his sight again, top lip rising, making his eyes narrow, showing as much respect as he thought the other boy deserved, and the urge to spit again took over. He gathered as much saliva as he could in his mouth, made sure his eyes were still on Maddox then spat onto the pavement.

Now it was Maddox's turn to narrow his eyes, saying to Davidson while shaking his head, "I can't do this."

"You already agreed. If you have a problem with it, I'm sorry but there's no turning back. Now, I'm going to leave and go back to my office. You'll be left alone with a few of my guards. When I come back, we'll go over what to say to your district. Try not to kill each other."

Mayor Davidson then straightened his shirt, placed his hands on his belt, and began walking off back to his office, whistling as he went, and Conrad felt even more annoyed, being reminded of Timothy.

"Hey," snapped Conrad, looking over his shoulder. "Why are there more guards around me?" No answer. Except for more of the annoying whistling, which slowly began to fade away. He decided trying to get an answer from the mayor was beyond pointless, so he simply squared his shoulders and looked over to the other boy again, who stood with the tips of his fingers in his pockets, fondly staring at the sky.

His vision abruptly darted to Conrad, the calm, uncaring look in his eyes soon transforming into disgust. Conrad made up his mind to be the first one to speak instead of letting the canid open his mouth first.

"What are you doing here? Can't you stay where you belong?"

"You mean in the fancy neighborhood I live in, now? Yeah, I guess I could do that." He shrugged one shoulder. "But why miss out on aggravating all you foul-tempered pyroglees? It's too much fun." He snickered, shaking his head. "I was told by the government in my city that I was needed in this wasteland. That I was the best choice because of my past. I thought we were going to simply talk about expanding our lands, making bigger living arrangements. Not any of this other nonsense."

"And you really thought they'd picked you to help with that?" Conrad snorted, arms now crossed.

"Oh, why don't you just-"

"Look, I don't know what happened to you that makes them think you can help unite pyroglees and canids, but I'm kind of curious to see if this works. I'm not telling you to be my friend or anything-God, no-but if this is what it takes to get under Bertram's skin, I'm all in."

"Bertram and that stupid anarchist, Kit." Maddox kicked at the ground, a growl coming out at Kit's name. "He's going to wish he never messed with me…or my parents."

"Hmm." Conrad briefly remembered when Kit came to visit their school on Buzzard. How on their way there, they came upon Maddox who stood in front of a classroom instead of being out on the field for P.E. where he was supposed to be. The boy breathed heavily in and out his nose, eyes shooting out fiery rays at the visiting vigilante. He even told them to ask Kit what Gift he had, though Conrad had a feeling he already knew. Which turned out to be nothing.

The truth became apparent after Kit decided to punish Ethan, who actually brought up the fact of the man having no Gift in front of the entire class. The man didn't try to defend himself in any way, or show everyone what power he held, only forcing his brother to work with the energy draining shield a few times in a row.

"I was wondering why he always had on those protective pads and shin guards like some kid competing on a team," Ethan grouched when they were inside their dorm room at the end of the day. "This guy really thinks he's something. I bet if he didn't have all that armor on, he'd be hiding under stuff, trying to get out of the way. Freakin' coward'." Conrad stopped an amused grin from climbing up his face as soon as Maddox opened his mouth to speak again.

"This is not going to be easy." The other boy's hand flew to the side of his head as he took a step back. "I don't know anyone in our town who wants to join sides with you pyroglees...or even be near a pyroglee. They're going to think I'm a traitor."

"You and me both," said Conrad, thinking about all the resentment he'd receive when they would hear him talking about uniting with the canids. "But I'm at least willing to try."

Maddox remained silent for more than a couple of seconds, ocean blue eyes on Conrad, his jaw moving from side to side as if he were gritting his teeth. Finally, he shrugged, kicked at the ground again, and said, "Fine, pyroglee. I guess I am too."

"Good, you two." Mayor Davidson came back onto the square. He clapped his hands together, a tooth bearing smile on his face. "Now that we've come to an agreement, we can finally get started on talking to your townspeople. Sort of, get them to see our strategy." He waved his hands around like he was signaling to someone, and since his eyes didn't fall on the two boys he'd been addressing, Conrad's defenses rose once again.

The quick steps of footprints on the cement, someone tightly grabbing his arm, gruffly telling him to get a move on. That was all Conrad needed.

Frustration already mounted to as high as it could get, he swung around and landed his fist onto the guard's chest, a burst of air coming out of the man's mouth along with a grunt as he stumbled backwards. More footsteps coming from his right and behind him let him know to hunch over so as not to be caught between them.

A cry of pain from another guard had him twist his head to the far left, where Maddox, his sharp teeth bared and claws poking out of his fingertips, threw a man into another, making them both crash onto the ground. Maddox wasn't finished. He then stretched out an arm to the left of himself, clutching a guard who tried to sneak up on him by his neck, and flinging him to the back of the square.

Surprisingly, Conrad didn't hear any words of protest from Davidson, not saying anything to try to get them to stop. Instead, the man remained quiet, hands on his hips, the beginnings of a smile sprouting up his face, even as Conrad stepped on a guard's arm who tried to grab his leg.

When it appeared no one else would come out to attack them, Conrad stayed in the same spot, unmoving, noticing Maddox didn't move either.

Their eyes met for a few seconds before they turned to the mayor, who seemed more than happy to have their attention.

"Huh," said Davidson, nodding. "I'll count that as teamwork." Conrad rolled his eyes at the same time Maddox let out a groan, just the thought of them working together sounding vile. But, if anything, he would make the most of it, even if part of his job required convincing other pyroglees why they should join forces with the Canids.

Chapter Three: Standing Together

Mayor Davidson had them hide in one of the clothing stores in the square while the townspeople were brought back out, confused and some of them angry that their shopping had been interrupted.

"Everyone gather around," said Davidson, only satisfied until the townspeople were more than a few feet away from him, leaving a small gap. "What you're about to learn today, is the value of joining together. Coexisting as an unstoppable unit, joining forces so we'll be a more powerful group."

"What are you talking about?" said a man in the front of the crowd. "We already are a strong unit. It's Bertram who needs to watch out for us!" He pumped a fist in the air, a cheer erupting from the crowd. Davidson patted at the air, meaning for them to settle down.

"While strong," continued Davidson. "We can be so much more if we simply stopped fighting with the canids." Silence. An abrupt silence falling on the square as soon as Davidson said the word canids. Conrad feared for the mayor's safety. "Now, I have brought someone whose mother meant a lot to this town. And not just him, but a canid he's grown close to." Conrad groaned and swiped a hand down his face, having had just about enough of Davidson and his multiple lies. When would it end?

Davidson briskly motioned to the store Conrad and Maddox were put inside, meaning for them to come out. Conrad rolled his neck around his shoulders, hearing two cracks sound between his shoulder blades. Maddox smoothed his shirt, exchanging a look with Conrad. They both nodded then stepped out onto the square.

Some of the townspeople's eyes grew wide when they saw Conrad, nudging each other and pointing at him. The others merely narrowed their eyes at Maddox, and Conrad cringed, knowing the other boy wasn't one to take disrespect lightly.

"You brought a canid to our town?" demanded the man who'd spoken first. "They're nothing but *foul* creatures who should stay in their own lands."

"They don't even like each other!" shouted someone from the middle of the crowd, who noticed the distance the boys kept from each other.

"Foul creatures?" Maddox spat, eyes locked on the man who insulted him. "The only foul creature I see is the one standing in front of me. Yeah, I'm talking to you, pyroglee."

"Shut up," murmured Conrad, shaking his head, a roar from the crowd taking over the man's infuriated cries.

Maddox turned to Davidson, snarling, "I'm out of here." As soon as he turned around to leave, the man Maddox got into an argument with whirled his hands around each other, a dark grey smoke rising into the air.

"Don't!" Conrad yelled just as the man flung the crackling fire straight towards Maddox. Without even thinking about it, Conrad took off, arm outstretched and hand wide open. He managed to stop the soaring flames in place before they could get any closer, intense heat engulfing his entire hand. But as much as he enjoyed the flames creating what he considered a blanket of warmth around his fingers, he didn't even try stopping the wrath building inside himself.

"Why would you do that?" snapped Conrad, sure his irises were on the brink of turning blood red…if they weren't there already. "You bring shame to our town, by acting like a *jerk* who can't even control his own Gift!?"

"He shouldn't even be here-" rambled the fire throwing man, stumbling over his words.

"No," interrupted Conrad, hand still feeling like it was on fire. "The way I see it, you shouldn't even be here. The people of Cove already think we're some uncontrollable miscreants who don't deserve to be around them, or their families. And you're just proving them right."

"Absolutely," said Davidson, a big smile on his face and hands on his hips. "You see how harmful it is for us to act this way. Not able to control our tempers, getting into fights with others. This young man here demonstrates the importance of getting along."

Conrad wanted to tape the mayor's lips together, never being one to like when all the attention was on him, especially because somebody else made it that way.

"Are you sure this is going to work?" said a tall boy in overalls who Conrad recognized as Lauren's older brother, Aaron. "How do we even know the canids will accept us?" Mayor Davidson opened his mouth to answer, but Conrad interrupted him.

"They have to. Us joining together will throw Bertram off."

"And they'll listen to me," said Maddox, stepping forward. "They may not like it at first but I can convince them." More silence descended on the square, people exchanging unsure looks with whoever stood next to them. But, in under a minute, and to Conrad's relief, Aaron spoke up again.

"If this is what it's going to take to bring down the Swifts…" He nodded his head twice, and rubbed his hands together. "Then I'm in."

"I'm in, too," added Lauren quietly, and Conrad was sure she felt uncertain. Pretty soon, the entire square was filled with the voices of townsfolk yelling their support, how they were willing to form an alliance with the canids if it meant bringing down Bertram. Conrad never would have thought they'd come to this point, joining sides with their

enemies, but in the end, he knew it was for the best. Now, all they had

to do was go over to the other side of Refuse. And he wasn't sure how

accepting they would be to a small pyroglee.

...

The two-story apartment buildings, complete with balconies jutting

out from the top of them, reminded Conrad of the time him, Timothy

and Ethan made their way to the tough canid, Lionel and his gang,

stopping them before they could commit a bank robbery. Once again,

the curtesy of crime boss, Magnum, who Conrad knew actually

wanted to get him killed.

He could talk all he wanted about how he could have single-hand-

edly completed Magnum's insane tasks all by himself. No problem.

But if he were really being honest with himself, Conrad knew he

wouldn't even be around anymore without his brother's help.

Mayor Davidson chose not to come with them, saying he had duties

to take care of back at his office. Why he didn't just say he'd rather be as far away from the canid town as possible, Conrad didn't know.

But he didn't seem to have any misgivings about sending him along

to the dangerous town.

As before, he spotted young kids sitting on the balconies to their

apartments, swinging their legs as they conversed with their friends or

family members, not paying much attention to the two boys being es-

corted by guards to the town area.

Conrad didn't know where their mayor was as they entered the

town square, the area having the same build to it as the one for the py-

roglees. Shops encircled the small space, making a ring of clothing

stores and restaurants. Even having some vendors selling food cook-

ing on a grill, or clothes hanging on wires.

Conrad and Maddox were then instructed to go to the back of the

square and wait while the guards retrieved most of the townspeople.

Conrad had to admit, it was more of a comfort to be out in the open

then in a grubby store.

Conrad watched as a microphone on a stand was scooted in front of

Maddox, who looked at the guards in surprise, probably wondering

why he had to talk first. But a few seconds later, a high voice yelled into their own microphone, "My fellow townspeople! We have brought for you today what you may consider one of our greatest enemies." Conrad couldn't resist casting a glare at the man who wasn't as old as Davidson, black shades covering his eyes and wearing a grey overcoat over a long shirt with black pants. A necklace with a white feather hanging off the end of it was wrapped around his neck three or four times, Conrad couldn't tell, but he did notice the man's scraggly brown boots, almost reaching his thighs.

He began to shake his head, wondering if the man got dressed up just for them. The snide remarks from Timothy already played through his mind, and he stopped a grin from climbing up his face.

"Ladies and gentlemen, what you see standing before you is not just one of our own, but someone else from other lands. A pyroglee." Several gasps erupted from the townspeople, and Conrad's hands grew warm, almost hot, when a couple of the canids stepped forward, hands balling into fists.

"They're not wanted here!" growled someone from the very back of the group, a snarl escaping from his throat afterwards. About what he'd expected. Stretching out his arms, Conrad's eyes flicking back to the mayor, who simply regarded the angry townsfolk with a calm look on his face, no wrinkles on his forehead, lips formed into a straight line, and arms resting comfortably by his sides. If Conrad didn't know any better, he'd almost say the mayor couldn't care less about joining together with the pyroglees. That he felt okay with Bertram having control over all of them. Before he could say something, Maddox beat him to it.

"If you all would just listen to me, you might understand why this is so important! Nobody expects us to join together but to keep fighting like wild animals. This is only part of Bertram's plan. Separate the people everyone else sees as threats and have them hating each other. Keep them preoccupied so we don't turn against him. A Swift. The city's beloved leader."

"Interesting," said the younger mayor, rubbing part of his arm. "But I don't think it's safe to join sides with the pyro-"

"Can you just **shut up**?!" yelled Maddox, rising so he almost stood on the tips of his toes. *Thank you*, thought Conrad, glad he didn't have to shout insults at the mayor. "You're not listening. If you want to continue being Bertram's little lap dog then so be it, but the rest of us are going to stand up and fight. And if teaming up with the py-roglees is the only way to do it then so be it." A couple of the towns-people exchanged expressions of uncertainty with each other, others turning to the mayor for answers, but he just continued to stand statue still, a frown now engraved on his face.

"My parents would agree to this in a second, but they can't." Maddox's eyes narrowed. "You know why? When we were living in the forest with other canids, we were told to leave by Kit and one other vigilante. When they protested, Kit threatened them by pulling out a weapon. My dad stepped forward, raised his hand, telling him to calm down, but Kit fired a shot and got him right in chest." Maddox paused, eyes narrowed, scratching his foot across the ground. "My mother just about lost her mind after they killed him, and I now live with my aunt and uncle."

"You're Maddox Bernard," said a woman in the middle of the square, mouth opening wide in shock. Maddox simply nodded, and Conrad thought it was finally time he put a few words in.

"The rest of my townspeople have already decided to join this plan." He raised his voice, attempting to rise up a little straighter. "All we need is you." It took a couple of minutes, and Conrad was afraid they'd come to another standstill, but before he knew it, shouts of "I'm in," took over the square, and their mayor finally moved in his spot by taking two steps forward.

"Alright!" he said, raising his hands. "Everybody, calm down. I will contact Davidson and let him know of our decision. But in the meantime, you will continue to stay in this part of Refuse. Understood?" He got some head nods and a few shouts of 'Yes, sir!', to Conrad's utter relief.

He picked up his feet, heading to the vehicle which transported them to the canid area, thoughts of the ugly look of confusion on Bertram's face when he learned of their coming together. Upper lip scrunched up, eyes narrowed, informing the citizens of Cove about the new terror of pyroglees and canids, and how he and K.OR.E. would do their best to look out for them. Heh. They could try.

Chapter 4: An angry Grandmother

The ride out of the canid town took them simply ten minutes, Conrad

making sure his window was rolled all the way up, the wind annoying

him as it ruffled his black hair. Unfortunately, Maddox didn't feel the

same, his window rolled all the way down and his arm resting on top

of the window sill. He would have snapped at the other boy to also roll

his window up, but he figured the cool air only bothered *him*. Well,

what he considered to be cool air at seventy degrees was probably a hot

box to anyone else.

Their driver pulled into the town of the pyroglees, settling into a dirt patch a couple feet away from the houses. Conrad quickly unbuckled his seatbelt, opened the car door, prepared to jump out, but stopped himself when he didn't hear anything on his left. Maddox still sat unmoving in his seat, staring out the car window as if searching for something. Conrad paused, unsure of what to do, the words he wanted to say stuck in his head.

"You stuck on the seat or something?" Finally. Now all he had to do was wait for the immobile boy to respond.

"Very funny, pyroglee." Maddox turned his head until he looked directly at Conrad, removing his arm from the window sill. "I'm going back to the canids to discuss a few things. I have to ready myself."

"For *what*?" Conrad squinted, wondering what could possibly be so important back in the town they'd just exited.

"Something that's none of your business, pyroglee." He opened his mouth to say more, but paused, eyes darting to the side of himself. "Um…What is your name, again?" Conrad snorted then jumped onto the dirt, hand grasping the edge of the door.

"It's Conrad…canid." He closed the door at the same time a tiny smile appeared on Maddox's face, turning around and searching for his own car. He took the keys out of his pocket, pressing the unlock button and heading to the area where he heard a single honk. He jumped into the driver's seat as soon as he opened the door to the car, twisted the keys in the ignition then turning on the radio, a quick-step beat of an old country song blasting out of the speakers.

He drove back to Cove City in no time at all, glad he didn't hear a police siren behind him with an officer signaling for him to pull over. That was the last thing he needed. Their neighborhood extended only a block, medium sized houses forming a half circle, some of them painted a light yellow while some light blue and others all white. His eyes scanned the row of houses for his grandmother's house, and when he spotted the small home which looked like a cottage, and turned the car into the driveway. It was at that moment he could see the front door opening. If he didn't know what panic felt like before, he certainly could feel the slimy tendrils of the sensation sliding across his stomach.

Liz came out onto the driveway in comfortable, light grey sweat-pants, a blue blouse and a novel clinched in her hand, which Conrad had seen her read several times before. He shut the car off once Liz crossed her arms, not moving from beside the front door.

He sat behind the wheel a couple seconds longer, contemplating which excuse he should give this time, most likely one which didn't involve lying about taking the car, because it was pretty obvious at this point. Unless, of course, he wanted to make up the destination. Yeah, he could do that.

"Conrad Brookes!" shouted Liz, stomping a foot. Conrad unlocked the door and slipped out, prepared for the worse. "Taking your grand-father's car to drive to that pyroglee town." Shoot, so she knew any-ways. Conrad clasped his hands together then stretched his arms above his head, trying to appear nonchalant, as if he didn't care how much trouble he was in. He quickly made his way to the front door, Liz side-stepping in front of him so he was blocked from going inside.

Liz briskly snatched the keys out of his hand, which he hadn't even realized he had still been holding. "Why are you going down there?" she demanded, tapping her foot.

"I wasn't at the stupid pyroglee town," Conrad snapped, moving to the side in an attempt to get pass Liz, but she merely blocked him off again.

"Don't lie to me, Conrad Brookes. I know that's where you go because someone's seen you driving off to Refuse."

"Who-?" Conrad thrust up his hands, ready to burn the lips off the person who couldn't mind their own business.

"It doesn't matter who it was, I just want to know why you've been going down there. Who are you meeting up with?" He continued to stare into her eyes, wracking his brain for what to say that wouldn't land him in hot water. Or, if he was being honest with himself, ice cold water.

"I just like to meet with people like me. That's it."

"And you couldn't tell me about any of this? Not to mention the fact you're blatantly taking your grandfather's car. Don't become like her-"

"Like who?" Conrad snapped, attempting to clear his mind, but the storm of thoughts just wouldn't go away. "And If somebody around here can't keep their eyes on something else then tell them they can come with me next time. And tell them to bring a lighter. The burning flesh of a snitch smells good."

The slap to his face came hard and fast, a stinging on his cheek only adding on to the pain. Conrad had his head down, worried about the fury he'd burst into if he looked up. Not sure if the whole house would catch on fire if he simply glanced at it. Liz had never hit him before, and he didn't know what to make of it, breathing coming out haggard as if he'd just been involved in a fist fight.

"Now, you're leaving for that school tomorrow," said Liz in a low tone of voice, and Conrad could practically feel her glare burning into his skull. "I don't know what they're teaching you up there, but I hope they can knock some sense into you." A long, mournful sigh burst from her mouth before she continued. "'Don't become your father', is what I should've said. Boy, just don't do it. You have your own life to live. Don't mess it up."

When Conrad finally whipped his head back up, he made sure his eyes looked directly at the door, confident if he looked at Liz, he'd see a tear sliding down her cheek. He reached out an arm to the doorknob, relieved when Liz moved out of the way to let him through.

He stormed through the cozy house which didn't seem as if he be-longed in it. Not with the stark white walls, some framed pictures of a scenic escape. One picture being a trail winding through eucalyptus trees, their branches blocking the sky. Conrad didn't want to see another woodland area, not liking anything that reminded him of Buzzard Island, the place his school rested on top of. He didn't mind completing schoolwork or studying for tests, but to go to a place built by Warren Swift almost made him want to go back to jail. Heck, he'd even sit inside the cell in Magnum's workplace the man had built specifically for him.

Magnum...If Conrad ever saw the crime boss again, he couldn't be sure what would happen to him. They'd dealt with two of his henchmen last year on Buzzard, but Conrad had a feeling that wasn't the last of them. The crime boss wasn't one to let things go, and if he wanted something bad enough, he'd have it handed to him in a second, even if it meant tearing down the entire city to do so.

Chapter Five: The Long Bus Ride

"Breaking News: A young man by the name of Maddox Bernard, along with his cousin and a few of their friends, have gone missing from their homes in Yellow Ridge, California. The others who are also missing, names are, Griff Malcolm, Jessie Swanson, Anthony Bernard, Danny Strider, and Streeter Jones.

Their parents beg anyone to help find them. Their disappearance was so unexpected and shocking, so please be on the look-out for them. One of their parents would like to make a statement." She began ushering a blond woman forward, who was constantly sniffling.

"Lacy Becket," the newswoman began. "Do you have anything to say about your daughter's disappearance?"

"Yes, I certainly do," she sniffled. "I recently adopted Jessie. And she was such a good daughter. She cut some of her hair off but began growing it back to its beautiful length."

Crawling out of bed the next morning, with a giant rock feeling as if it were planted in his stomach, had never been more difficult, his thoughts continually going back to what he was about to do. His plan to escape didn't seem so daring anymore. Not since the news of Maddox's disappearance blasted out of the radio and T.V. stations.

Jerk. He just had to be first, didn't he?

He didn't say anything to his grandmother even though she occasionally glanced up from her plate to look at him, studying him, seeming as if she wanted to ask a question but holding back. Finally, she put down her fork and straightened in her seat, clasping both hands together as if they were suddenly at a business meeting.

"Look here, boy," she began, eyes boring into him. "Don't be getting into any trouble at school, now."

"I'm *not*," Conrad grouched, quickly wiping his hands off on his napkin.

"And don't be running off doing anything dangerous. Do you hear me?" This time, Conrad merely nodded, chewing the last of his pancakes which he knew Liz had spent most of the early morning making. The fact she'd gone through so much trouble making his breakfast only filled him with more guilt, the honking of the bus providing a huge bucketful of relief. He threw his fork down, jumped out of his seat, and rushed to the door, but something stopped him, turning him around slowly so he was facing his grandmother again.

He made his way over to Liz, hesitated, then wrapped an arm around her shoulders, making sure to pull her in tight. The warm texture of her cheek rubbed against his own, and he spun back around as soon as another honk sounded from outside.

"Alright, I'm coming!" Conrad barked as soon as he got the front door open, pushing it closed when he stormed outside. He then hopped off the porch, trying to ignore the driver of the van beckoning to him frantically, meaning for him to hurry up.

Once he got to the van's doors, their driver, who had on his same

42

black shades, propped a clipboard onto the steering wheel, pen held above it.

"Name?" He asked in his snippy voice, dyed brown hair fading off his scalp.

"Conrad Brookes." As soon as he spoke, Conrad jumped onto the steps leading up into the van, not caring if the man thought he was clear or not, simply making his way forward. Kids sat on the peeling, leather seats which looked as if they needed to be redone, or at least replaced. He could feel side glances of kids who didn't want to look him in the face, only getting their quick stares in.

Seated in the middle row, inspecting an open binder he had on his lap and wearing a new pair of loafers, was Timothy, red hair sparking from the electricity he probably had churning in the strands. He sat at the very edge of his seat, taking up most of the space, legs crossed and humming to himself. Conrad came to an impatient stop next to him, impatiently tapping his foot. Timothy finally glanced up, saying in his nasal voice, "Oh! Greetings, Mighty Mouse-" He observed his stance, already round eyes growing wider. "Or...somewhat taller, Mighty Mouse. Are there new concoctions which spur on the growth cycle Locke doesn't know about?"

"Just get out of the way." Conrad waited while he scooched next to the window then plopped down on the cool surface, dropping his backpack onto the floor. He turned his head to Timothy in annoyance when the other boy's stare lingered on him, not going away no matter how fierce his glare was.

"If you don't stop," Conrad growled, shaking his head. "I'm gonna-"

"Locke apologizes but the science behind it is mindboggling. Just think about it. You're almost-"

"Taller than you? Yeah, I know." Timothy blew out a puff of air, snapping the binder shut.

"Well, Locke wouldn't go *that* far, but it's pretty close."

Conrad sighed and slid down in his seat, making sure to close his eyes as soon as the van started moving. He planned to ignore the other boy all the way to the docks, getting comfortable before he fell asleep. There was no noise in their van, no loud talking aloud despite the fact he was seated next to Mr. Loudmouth himself. They were on the vehicle where the true bad kids resided, where not one of them could say they hadn't been dragged on the first year in handcuffs.

Ethan thought he had done something wrong to end up where he was

but oh, no. Warren was just being a jerk. At least, that's the way Con-

rad saw it.

Chapter Six: Beverly

As soon as the van took a turn onto the freeway, he sat back in his seat and relaxed, not looking forward to the bouncing boat ride to their school, the splashing of waves inside his head making him feel sick, and they hadn't even boarded yet.

"Almost there," the driver yelled, the smell of salt water blowing through an open window, making Conrad feel queasy. He could only imagine what he'd feel like on the actual boat, itself, if only the irritating scent of the docks hurt his head. Now that he thought about it, he should be fine as long as he stayed in his cabin, unmoving, eyes tightly shut, and as long as no one bothered him.

He closed his eyes, but only for a little while, pretending to be fast asleep, hoping no one would bother him. As soon as the van began slowing down, Conrad already knew they reached their destination in no time at all, the minutes seeming to go by like they were merely seconds. Maybe he shouldn't have closed his eyes.

"We're nearing the parking lot so prepare to leave the van. Grab all your stuff and only unbuckle your seatbelts when we're parked."

Conrad sat up in his seat, observing the buildings which passed by the window, some a dark brown and tall while others were squat with bright colors like sunflower yellow or sky blue. People scurried down the sidewalks in bathing suits or summer clothes, clutching bags and a drink by their sides, occasionally talking on a cell phone. A chilly breeze drifted to his side of the van, making him want to blow a hole through the roof out of frustration.

"Roll it *up*," he growled, thinking Timothy had to be the one with his dang window down, letting in unwanted air.

"Oh, I'm sorry. I didn't know it was bothering you." A girl with mocha brown hair who looked to be the same age as Conrad, and wearing a tank top with jean shorts began pushing the window next to her closed, displaying a smile at him when she finished. The girls skin color also happened to be almost as dark as Ethan's, bringing out the dark brown, almost black color in her hair.

He recognized her as Beverly Jones, someone he sometimes saw out on the field on Buzzard Island, laughing and joking around with her friends. All of a sudden, he didn't know what to do with himself, so he simply shrugged then said quietly, "Thanks," almost mumbling his words. He tried to smile back at her, but all he managed to do was slightly push the left side of his lip up. He eventually gave up, turning forward in his seat again with arms crossed, a giggle reaching his ears.

He didn't know how, but he had somehow made her laugh, and he couldn't help but feel somewhat proud of himself, glad Ethan wasn't the only one who could make a girl smile.

He stretched his legs out once the van exited the freeway, zooming down a few more blocks before pulling into the driveway holding the rest of the vehicles.

"Alright, everybody," commanded the driver as he pulled into a parking spot. "Get out of your seats and form a line down the middle of the van. Then follow me as we head to the docks." A few kids grumbled to themselves as they woke up from their naps, tired and in no mood to be taking a stroll to Pier Thirty-Five.

Just like the driver said, they all formed, or squished, into a long line, some of kids in the back remaining seated, waiting for their turn to get up. With the driver's command, they then exited the van, the breeze even more bothersome now that they were near the docks, the cool weather plus the ocean smell making Conrad's head swirl. He was back in his worst nightmare. He wished to be at a campfire, or any fire for that matter, allowing the flames to roll up his arms, the soothing sensation it created taking his mind away from where they were headed.

Waves splashed against part of the beach, flinging bits of leaves, or kelp, into the air. Ahead of them, kids formed a long line on the dock, their boat, Blue Waves, waiting for them to enter.

"So, I know your name," spoke someone from the side of him. "But I never did get anything else." Beverly walked comfortably beside him, swinging her backpack, the same smile on her face. Conrad sighed, the beachy setting really putting a damper on his mood.

"Like what?" he grumbled, another gust of wind blowing around them. He shivered and pulled the hood on his jacket so it sat on top of his head, knowing he probably looked like some kind of hooligan. He didn't care, wishing the people who scurried past them would keep their eyes ahead and simply ignore the school kids walking by them.

"Like, where are you from? And how did you end up going to Buzzard Island?" Beverly shrugged, keeping her eyes straight forward.

"I grew up on the East side of Cove City. And how did I end up going to this place? Don't know. Guess they don't like who raised me."

"And who would that be?" Beverly eyed him curiously, eyebrows furrowed.

"You *don't* need to know that." Conrad shoved his hands in his pockets, growing irritated. Beverly nodded, then looked down, no longer staring at him. He couldn't help but feel a little bit bad, like he had pushed a homeless dog out of his way or threw a cat out a window. If only she'd close her dang eyes or look someplace else.

Not being able to take it anymore, her downcast eyes grating at his soul, Conrad blurted out, "You'll find out eventually, alright?

Sometime this year." To his relief, Beverly finally looked at him again, the same cheerful giggle bursting out her throat. The line to the boat moving forward couldn't have served as a bigger relief to him, not really knowing what else to say to the girl he had thought got her feelings hurt but actually just brushed off his outburst like it was nothing.

"I'll see you inside, fire boy," she said as they neared the ramp going up to the inside of the boat, flipping hair over her shoulder. The best response he could do was nod then quickly look away, though he wasn't really sure why he looked away, the whole situation not just strange to him but also interesting. And the fact that she knew what kind of Gift he had, whether from asking about him on the field or she just could tell, he didn't know, but he couldn't stop the curiosity from growing inside of himself.

Chapter Seven: A Delightful Distraction

"Form a straight line," said the captain impatiently to the students

who arrived near the entrance to the boat, waving her hands so they

opened and closed. If Conrad didn't feel squished before, he now

knew what a squashed bug felt like as more students pushed to form

the line which would keep them out of trouble.

Fog floated in the air, thick so it blocked out some of the scenery in

front of them. Conrad didn't mind. The less he saw of the ocean the

better. It was bad enough he had to smell the salt water, the fishy

aroma drifting through his nostrils like the stench of rotten eggs,
strong and absolutely disgusting.

It soon came time for their group to board, and Conrad simply
breathed through his mouth, not letting anymore of the foul stench
into his nose.

"Come on. Hurry up," urged the captain, growing impatient, getting
on Conrad's nerves. They were going as fast as they dared. What
more did she want from them? Actually, it would probably make her
very happy to hand them a detention slip for moving too fast, making
sure they arrived at school on the principal's bad list, which was the
last the last thing he needed.

As soon as he walked by the impatient woman, her nose turned up at
him and eyes narrowed, apparently knowing what Gift he had, most
likely hearing about it from teachers at his school who warned her to
watch out for him. He didn't need others to watch out for him, but if
they wanted to turn their noses up at him then he could show them
something to be afraid of. All he had to do was call his Gift, feel the
heat rushing into his hands, and blast whoever made him mad into
oblivion. In fact, he could already feel his Gift start to heat up, the

warmth rushing to his head as well, nearly blurring his vision.

He never knew a time when his Gift made such a rapid appearance, swirling through his insides in a wild melee. The captain opened her mouth and gasped, noticing his eyes now changed color to a threatening blood red. But before he even had a chance to do anything, like burn the captain's hair off her head, the clomping of footsteps reached his ears, and someone immediately grasped his shoulder.

"Come on, Conrad. Everyone's waiting," said a soft voice. The grip on his shoulder soon going to his hand, interlocking their fingers.

The heat began to slowly cool down as soon as he realized who took his hand. Beverly nodding at him before looking back inside the boat, lifting his hand, and pulling him to two seats by a window.

Conrad slowly turned his head to look at Beverly as soon as they sat down, then down at their hands, which they still had clasped together.

"Oh," she said in surprise before taking her hand back. "I thought you may have needed a little help. If not, sorry for catching you off guard." Before he even knew what was happening, Conrad managed to get two words out.

"No. Thanks."

She flicked her hair off her shoulder, looked at him in concern, and said, "Does that happen often? Having your Gift about to burst out like that?" He shrugged, looking her straight in the eye.

"Yeah, sometimes."

"And you can't control it?"

"Depends on how mad I get."

"She made you mad?" Beverly pointed at the lady letting the rest of the kids in. "Why?"

"She looked at me funny." He crossed his arms as her own eyes widened, her lips separating in a mini gape. He may have been talking to a girl for a good amount of time, but he suddenly regretted ruining it because he couldn't keep his words to himself.

Beverly shook her head, hair flopping back and forth onto her shoulders. "You should be the one with the tough sounding middle name and not me. I'm hardly a rebel. Plus, my hair..."

Conrad continued to stare at her for a few moments before saying, "You dye it that color?"

"Yep, and for the first time, too." She ran her fingers through some strands, beaming at him as if she'd performed a complicated magic trick.

The boat's horn blasted, signaling it was time to take off. Conrad snapped his eyes closed, the rocking of the boat turning his head in circles, throwing his thoughts out of whack, making him more un-comfortable than he already was.

"Start talking about…fire," He instructed, moving his fingers to-wards himself as if he wanted to let her in on a secret.

"Okay, um…" She made a fist before placing her chin on it, elbow perched on her knee. "You ever been on a camping trip? I can make the best fires by summoning the wind. It's actually really easy. All I have to do is concentrate on the air around me."

Conrad had to admit, he was glad he got her to talk about about fire, steering his thoughts away from the ocean and the waves crashing into the sides of the boat. The distraction was exactly what he needed in a time where they were about to dare the open waters. He didn't even know where his brother went, having had lost track of him as soon as he started talking to Beverly. Not that he minded. Being free of the other boy put him at ease, not having to hear his big mouth a comfort. But it didn't last long.

56

"Locke feels like our passage to the most joyful place on Earth is nearly at an end," said Timothy, sitting up in his seat, stretching his arms above his head.

Chapter Eight: A way to Escape

"Don't listen to him," grouched Conrad, scooting down in his seat.

"He goes on talking about nothing because he enjoys it."

"Timothy Locke," said Beverly, cocking her head to the side. "Do

you know Nova Bringham?" Conrad wanted to smack his backpack

against his head, wondering what is was going to take to shut them

up.

"Possibly." Timothy tilted his head back and squinted his eyes.

"You may see us a bunch of times this year, depending on if our agreement is still in effect. Why?"

Beverly shrugged, swiping a strand of hair off her shoulder.

"Oh, just curious." Conrad watched as a small grin crept up her face, her eyes looking to the ground at the same time.

Conrad turned his head to glance at Timothy, the other boy doing the same so their eyes eventually met, both confused by Beverly's question. Suddenly, it hit Conrad head on what the girl was getting at. NO. She couldn't possibly be serious. He looked at the floor then back at Timothy, unable to accept what she meant.

Their long boat ride to Buzzard now seemed as if it would take forever now that his brother had something else to be smug about.

"Alright, everyone!" called a man in a security guard outfit who came out of the captain's cabin. "We have a little more ways to go, so no getting up and walking around. Stay in your seats until we reach the dock. Understood?" All the students on the boat dutifully called out "Yes!", not wanting to be the one who got on the security guard's bad side and spend the whole first week of school in detention.

Not looking to keep his eyes open any longer, Conrad slowly drifted off to sleep, trying his best to ignore the sound of the waves hitting the sides of the boat, making it sway somewhat from side to side. Ugh. A camping trip and a nice, big campfire sounded really nice all of a sudden, a fire which would warm his hands and caress his fingers, the smoke creating a comforting blanket around him.

A sharp poke on his arm jolted him awake, his thoughts of a warm campfire diminishing into thin air. It took all he had not to burst into a ball of flames, scorching the entire boat until it became nothing but ash floating on the water.

It didn't help the security guard who'd woken him up still stood over him with arms crossed, a frown on his face. Conrad had just about enough.

"Okay, I'm awake!" He tried to keep his voice low but it came out as a shout anyway. "What more do you want from me?" He briefly wondered if the tall man who stood in front of him was the same guard who got on Ethan's nerves the first two times they went on the boats. If so, Conrad didn't know how he would keep his Gift from bursting out.

"I'm just making sure everyone is prepared to disembark," said the guard with an upturned nose, eyes narrowed and lips pursed.

If Conrad had to see someone else with an uppity look on their face, he knew flames would burst out his hands. He directed his eyes at the ground, not wanting to upset Beverly by yelling at the man in front of him. And like a breath of fresh air, the man finally moved away from him to another area of the boat, probably because he could tell Conrad was about to go off. At least, that's what Conrad liked to think.

"Look, there it is," said a boy wearing a baseball cap, pointing at the window behind him. Out on the bluish green water, lay Buzzard Island, Oak trees poking out of the center of it, the leaves a tropical green color and the branches stretched out like long arms.

Conrad could see the wind pick up whichever leaf had fallen on the ground and whirl them around so they danced in the air, skipping on air currents or sometimes floating on the water. A beeping up above his head let him know they were getting closer to the dock, and he became a little light headed when the boat's engines slowed their pace.

"Finally," said Beverly, peering at the island through a window. "I need something to eat besides these snacks they give us." Conrad couldn't agree with her more as his own stomach let out an impatient grumble.

The guard quickly made his way to the only door which would let them out, the boat coming to a complete stop, propellers no longer flinging up water. They were then instructed to form another line down the middle of the boat.

"Everybody keep moving," yelled the guard, waving his hands above his head. "As soon as we make it outside, we're going to wait for one of your teachers to show up. And after that, you already know the rest."

They quickly excited the boat, greeted by cool air and a partly sunny sky, a cloud blocking half of the sun. That's just what he needed. Something else to remind him he hated going to Buzzard Island so much. He craved the hot air back at Cove City, a place where he rarely had to wear a jacket.

He rubbed his arms, waiting for the dang teacher who'd take them to the Administration building before sending them off to the dorms to show them where their rooms were, although Conrad felt pretty certain he knew exactly where to go. Just straight forward on the dirt trail, to the large fence that seemed to be as tall as some of the eucalyptus trees, a reminder why trying to escape would only end up with their inevitable capture. Conrad huffed at the thought of it, figuring

there were other ways to get off the island and head back to the city.

Chapter Nine: Growth Spurt

Actually, he didn't have to guess. He already knew.

"Hello, hello!" came a cheerful shout of someone walking their way, and Conrad turned his head to the right to see Ms. Gail speed-walking towards them in black pants and a matching cardigan jacket with beige buttons reaching her neck. Her dyed black hair was flung over her shoulders so it flopped against her back, hair pins holding it back so it didn't get in her face.

"All the students on this boat are accounted for and have been checked in," said the security guard, nodding. "You can take them back to their rooms while we get ready to set off again to pick up the remaining kids." *I'm sure she already knows that,* Conrad thought, irritated at the man who must have thought they were all clueless.

Ms. Gail merely gave the man a toothless smile before turning back to the students, clasping her hands together.

"Keep close together as we start making our way to the dorms. And you, my good man." She turned to the security guard. "You may now depart. Thank you for keeping an eye on all the students and making sure they arrived safely. Farewell, sir." The man nodded, cocking his head to the side, but not before giving her a strange look. Conrad couldn't figure out why at first until he really thought about it. Their science teacher came off as a little strange to people who weren't used to her, and he had to admit, their teacher seemed a little weird to him, too. She always came off as uncomfortable, like something strong gripped her in the back, pinching her skin between its fingers. Without saying another word, she swiveled around before marching back on the path she came down on, occasionally looking over her shoulder to see if everyone followed and hadn't wandered off.

The students picked up their feet, following the quick step woman as best as they could without tripping over their own two feet or the overgrown roots which poked out of the ground.

Ahead of them, Conrad observed the concrete wasteland, its layers of cement piled together, windows implanted into them, and wooden doors complete with golden door knobs below the glass. He could picture the students residing in their rooms, smacking on chips or listening to music on headphones. They only were supposed to bring three things with them to school, but Conrad didn't bother, simply bringing his backpack along with pencils and paper. He didn't need anything else. He already had a plan to collect his other tools when he made it back into the city. He just had to be patient.

Before long, they made it to the administration building, Conrad's feet sore from the long walk on the terrain. Sitting down and getting comfortable on his bed became a fervent want, that and getting something to eat.

Kids playing their daily game of soccer raced by him, kicking a ball, sending it racing towards the net. Another group of kids sat in a circle on the field, speaking in low voices, leaning close together so their shoulders touched. A few of them looked up at him as he came closer then quickly looked away once he cast them a dirty look, not in the mood to be on display for anybody.

Their cafeteria hunched on the ground, giving the appearance of a frog, it's two windows serving as the eyes, the front door it's open mouth. A yard duty teacher stood next to a wooden table with plastic plates on its surface, sizzling hot dogs on all of them. Conrad sped his way to the table without even thinking about it, the aroma of the food making his stomach growl. Once the yard duty teacher handed him a plate, he shoved part of the hot dog into his mouth, savoring the meaty goodness topped with ketchup drizzling down the side.

Someone whistled across from him, seeing red hair and another person with brown hair cut shorter than when he first attended school, no longer sporting an afro. Conrad would have turned and joined them but the smell of food was too much. He didn't have to guess who had ran over to join him, the skidding of shoes on the grass alerting him to both Ethan and Timothy, their backpacks high on their shoulders, Ethan smacking on mint flavored gum.

It felt kind of weird for him seeing Ethan at the school so early, especially since his boat arrived before his.

"What did Locke tell you, Boss Man? A growth spurt concoction. It's the only explanation."

"I mean," said Ethan, glancing at Conrad with narrowed eyes. "He grew up a *little*."

"You two, huh?" A rare grin sprouted up Conrad's face, enjoying their disbelief at his height, which happened to be five foot seven inches.

"Yeah, me too," snapped Ethan, tilting his head to the side. "Whatever you're doing, man, I need to get started on it. I can't believe this."

Conrad wanted to continue the conversation about how tall he was, but the shrieking of the bell meant they had to head off to the dorms. Tomorrow morning would be his first subject, which happened to be History with Mr. Grey, Ethan's least favorite class. It wasn't like Conrad, himself, hoped to be enthralled by learning about what happened in the past, but it was taught by his favorite teacher.

Chapter 10: The Breakup

Once they made it into The Concrete Wasteland, Conrad immediately
went to the two hundreds buildings, only slowing down when the cor-
rect classroom came into his line of sight.

He immediately put his hand around the doorknob, thrusting the
door open before stepping inside the room which had a war memora-
bilia feel to it. All along the walls were posters of people in old,
scratched up clothes, dirt stained on the sleeves or, in direct contrast,
a woman in a fancy long dress, posing in front of a mansion.

Their teacher, Mr. Grey, sat at his desk with a stack of papers beside a desktop computer, a pair of scraggly black glasses on his ears.

Conrad had a feeling the moment their teacher looked up, it would be like staring into the eyes of a hawk. A vicious, flesh-eating hawk. To anyone else, that may have been unnerving, but to Conrad, it suited him just fine.

He picked a seat in the front row, comfortable at being in Mr. Grey's direct line of site. Ethan and Timothy, on the other hand, chose seats in the middle row. Though, in Conrad's opinion, he thought they should have sat all the way in the back, so Mr. Grey couldn't hear their big mouths.

As more students came in and sat in their seats, their teacher scooted his chair back, lifted his glasses up with just his thumb, waited a few more seconds then said, "Alright, now that everyone's seated, we can get started with today's lesson. Since we already went into great detail about some of this city's bad guys, let's talk about the good. Warren in particular and Bertram." Conrad fidgeted, suddenly uncomfortable.

"Who here can explain to me why Bertram is so important to Cove? Why do we need him?" Need him? Had Mr. Grey gone off the deep end? Did Conrad need to have his hearing checked? In the very front, all the way to the left, Kevin Sniderly spoke up.

"He protects us and our families. He makes sure no criminal goes unpunished and sits behind bars."

"Very good." Mr. Grey nodded, hand raised so he could call on somebody else, who happened to be another Swift lover. Mr. Grey seemed pleased yet again as if the student just answered a complicated math problem. Conrad frowned, wondering when their teacher became a Swift lover himself, when it occurred to him what may have happened. Their teacher might have gotten a strict warning about bringing up the Swifts in a bad light, and had been told about the consequences if he were to do so again.

Conrad scooted lower in his seat, shifting his eyes away from their teacher so he could look at his hands, at the lines swerving across them, not wanting to hear any more about the Swift's good deeds.

"Mr. Brookes, pay attention to what's being discussed," demanded Mr. Grey in a firm voice, surprising Conrad, who didn't think their teacher was paying any attention to him. "Or escort yourself out of my classroom." *Hmph.* He straightened himself and placed his hands on the desk, fingers clasped together, eyes directed at their teacher, not looking anywhere else.

Mr. Grey regarded him for a few more seconds as if trying to figure him out, to get a good read on him before he could cause any trouble. Without saying another word, Mr. Grey turned back around to the white board as best he could with his cane which reached his hip.

An hour later, the bell signaling the end of class gave out its' loud shriek, prompting all of the students to swipe their binders and pencils into their backpacks and jump out their seats. Conrad slung his own backpack on his shoulders, getting ready to leave, when a firm voice stopped him in his tracks.

"Conrad." He stopped in his tracks as soon as he heard Mr. Grey's voice. He looked at Ethan and Timothy, and swiped his hand to the side, meaning for them to go on ahead. The two boys walked to the door, sometimes throwing Conrad a confused look along the way. He finally stuffed his hands into his pockets, turning to face Mr. Grey as he did so.

"Something told me you are bound to set out on a little trip this year." Mr. Grey wiped at the white board with an eraser as he talked, his back to Conrad. Inside, he startled, looking to punch the idiot in the gut who told on him.

"If you do, remember to be extra careful…because I have a feeling, they're not going to be happy with you bringing those two back. No. Not at all." He erased one last word, and finally turned to face Conrad. "Especially the one-eyed-one." He swiveled back around to the board, marker capped again. "Now, hurry on to your next class."

Conrad walked out the door, Mr. Grey's voice playing through his head, curious as to how his teacher had any idea about his plans. Who else knew? Where they planning to stop him? No, Mr. Grey seemed content with just giving him a warning. So maybe he had a chance…

…

He never expected it to happen, always thinking his friend/brother could woo any girl by simply staring at them. On second thought, Eva didn't seem like the type of girl who'd settle with a nice guy. So, yeah. Maybe he shouldn't have been all that surprised.

Things had started out normally, their classes going by in a slow pace as if their teachers never wanted the day to end. But, lunch time was when things always went down, whether two students got into a shouting match with each other or someone being sent to the principal's office for misbehaving.

It didn't matter. Ethan strode off to the woods behind the field after lunch, Samantha keeping up with his quick speed, not allowing him to get away from her. Curious, Conrad stayed at a slower speed behind them, hearing Samantha talking in a loud voice as if someone offended her.

Walking into the beginning of the woods, he saw Ethan and Samantha standing next to each other, talking to someone. Well, Ethan was talking to someone. Samantha stood by with her arms crossed, eyes narrowed.

If he craned his neck, he could see who Ethan was talking to, and it happened to be his girlfriend, Eva, her brown hair curled and standing so her hip jutted out to the right. In the background stood someone Conrad could hardly see. A guy keeping a safe distance away from the arguing. As soon as they quieted down, Ethan whirled away from Eva, shaking his head. Samantha turned to follow after him, but not before coming to a halt, staring at Eva dead in the eye, and calling her a foul name. And in a second afterwards, Eva lunged forward and dug her fingernails into Sam's hair, pulling her head back.

Samantha let out a shriek before performing a half spin and grabbing the other girl by *her* hair, causing Ethan to turn around and sprint to the fighting girls. Conrad watched in amusement as Ethan separated the two girls, keeping them away from each other by using both of his arms.

Without warning, the other boy further out in the woods came forward, grabbing Ethan by the back of the shirt, pulling him backwards. Conrad almost felt sorry for the guy. Not even throwing a punch, Ethan simply grabbed him by the collar of his shirt before shoving him to the ground so he fell on his knees.

"What!?" Ethan twisted the guys collar, not letting him go. "Man, what?!" When the guy on the ground didn't do anything but stare wide-eyed at his aggressor, Ethan let him go, stomping away again. Eva didn't hesitate to cast a dirty look at her new boyfriend, who Conrad sometimes saw boasting about how strong he was.

Conrad ran next to Ethan, keeping up with his fast pace.

"That was interesting." Conrad kept the grin off his face as he spoke, but Ethan caught the amusement in his voice, anyways.

"Shut up." Against all odds, a laugh came out of Ethan's mouth, and Conrad relaxed somewhat, still unsure whether the other boy remained in an angry temperament.

"So, uh." He began, scratching the back of his head. "Samantha knew about this before the rest of us?" Shrugging, a disgruntled sigh coming out of his mouth, first, Ethan then glancing at him before saying, "She already knew beforehand. Some talk was going around or something.' He jabbed his foot on the ground. "These people and their big mouths."

He couldn't help but suspect his brother was hiding how he really felt, occasionally flicking his eyes at him in a quick side glance.

"Conrad." Ethan stopped, staring at him. "I'm fine, man." The best Conrad could do was nod and keep his mouth closed like someone taped it shut. Well, that answered his question, anyway…kind of, the sorrow in Ethan's eyes telling him a different story. He almost raised his hands up in joy when Samantha came next to Ethan, almost forgetting about all his plans he wanted to carry out. And they were going to be accomplished. No matter what.

Chapter 11: A Sad Truth

As soon as nighttime snuck into the school, the crescent moon flashing a gleeful smile at them amongst the stars, Timothy scrambled to get ready to go to the lab, grabbing a pencil and a bunch of papers from his backpack.

"You ready, Ethan?" asked Timothy, tugging his arms through the sleeves of jacket, and looking up at the clock on the wall.

"Yep." Ethan mumbled his answer, chewing on left over french toast he got from breakfast that morning. Conrad blinked, wondering if he heard him wrong.

"Wait, you guys are both going down there?" A snicker came out of his throat, counting all the ways they could get caught in his head. 1. A yard duty teacher walking into the lab to see if anything was amiss. 2. Ethan spraining his ankle on one of those rickety chairs as he tried to run away from an explosion Timothy let get out of control.

The annoying idea of joining them on their trek to the lab wouldn't leave his mind, screaming at him to exit the suffocating room and get out for a bit. To a place where desks weren't scattered everywhere around the room, or a long whiteboard had writings on it from a marker.

"I need to get out of this room for a bit." Ethan shrugged one shoulder. "They got us in here like we're in jail or something."

"Right-O, Boss Man," agreed Timothy, rummaging through his backpack. "Locke also needs some fresh air. And maybe a nice whiff of electric parts blown to smithereens."

Conrad heaved in air down his throat before letting it out in an agitated sigh.

"I'm going, too." Ethan and Timothy shared surprised expressions,

Timothy raising one eyebrow while Ethan squinted at Conrad. He even surprised *himself* when the words came out of his mouth.

"Alright, Conrad!" Timothy raised a hand in the air, curling it into a fist when he brought back down, again. "The more the merrier!"

"Yeah," Conrad grumbled once Ethan and Timothy opened the window, noticing one person had been missing from his bunkbed the entire time. "The more the merrier." He grabbed the window sill and pulled himself up, not looking forward to what was going to happen inside Timothy's beloved lab.

...

As usual, Timothy merely had to run his hand over a pad on the door for it to unlock itself, kicking his knees up in his usual prance. But as if colliding into a brick wall, Timothy came to a halting, shoes screeching across the ground, stop. Conrad only had to shift his eyes to the back of the room to understand why.

Seated at one of the tables, a leg lifted up so he could rest his black and white Converse sneaker covered foot on the chair he sat on, was none other than Gary, moving the point of his pencil on a sheet of paper.

Stomping his foot on the ground, Timothy began clapping his hands to get the other boy's attention. Gary slowly raised his head up, bored. "Hey!" exclaimed Timothy, stomping over to the table Gary sat at. "Locke thought we went over this. This is *his* time in the lab, not yours."

Conrad picked up his feet as soon as Ethan did, knowing he'd need help if he had to break them up from a fight. He chortled. Timothy and Gary in a fight. Timothy would win, obviously, but it would still be a funny thing to see. Reaching the table, Timothy's heated shouts crashed into Conrad's ears, ranting about their deal and how he had to follow it. Not paying any attention to him, Gary continued to sketch a picture of a woman, tears streaming down her eyes as a shadowy person approached her.

"You have to keep your part of the deal, man," explained Ethan in a lower tone of voice. *Always the calmer one.* It usually worked...until now.

"No." The lead to Gary's pencil flew across the paper, adding to the scared woman's hair.

"*No?*" snapped Ethan, twisting around after having been about to walk off. "Okay, man, listen, I'm not going to say this again. Get your stuff and get out." But the other boy wasn't having it, slamming his hands on the table, leaning forward, and really opening his mouth to exclaim, "NO!"

"Oh, really? Really?" snarled Ethan, also leaning forward so him and Gary were face to face. Conrad wouldn't have minded eating from a bag of popcorn at that moment, throwing some candy in his mouth as well, but simply sitting on a chair with his feet on the table provided more than enough comfort as he viewed the shouting match he thought would never happen. Even Timothy was struggling to hold in what had to be wild laughter, the sides of his lips shooting up before falling back down again.

Timothy's hand flew up to the wall he stood next to, banging the button which set one of the small objects into the air, performing front flips and side spins before hitting the ground. Conrad wanted to put on sunglasses as soon as the explosion rocked the floor, enjoying watching the flames lick the sides of the glass in a beyond hungry, he'd almost say starving, manner.

He almost didn't notice Gary duck under the table in fear, hiding even his sneakers from out of sight. Ethan simply kept his hands flat on the table, unmoving, the fire highlighting the aggravated frown on his face.

"You see?! You see?!" exclaimed Timothy after Gary crawled out from under the table then stormed out of the lab. "Nobody believed Locke when he told them, but the little rat has a bad side. *And* he doesn't listen. Well, now you've seen it with your own eyes!"

Glancing at the picture of the crying woman left on the table, Conrad didn't hesitate picking it up, studying the dark drawing. A sketch of a shadow coming up behind her, resembling another person, caught his eye, prompting him to ask, "Who is this?" Timothy became preoccupied with cleaning a table, wiping off the surface with the long sleeve of his shirt. Once finished, he crossed his arms, standing up straighter.

"His mother." He kicked out a chair from under a table then proceeded to sit down on it. "Though, Locke doesn't know why he draws her as the one who needs help, since she was the abuser." Conrad locked eyes with Ethan, both of them staring at each other in shock.

"Abuser?" Ethan raised his hands in the air, shaking them. "You're not telling me, man-"

"But Locke shouldn't say too much." Timothy jumped up, shaking his head. "Ms. Violet made him promise to keep his mouth shut, so that's what he's going to do."

Conrad stood still in the room which began to feel way too cramped, wondering if the little creep really had been abused. But even if he had, Conrad wouldn't let the crazy punk distract him, not in the slightest.

Chapter 12: Goodbye, Swift Kid

By the time lunch rolled around the next day, Conrad stiffly sat

down with his tray of a bag of potato chips, a slice of pepperoni pizza,

and a carton of milk at the usual spot he, Ethan, and Timothy went to.

Oh, yeah, and sometimes one more person.

'Smack!' Gary slammed his tray down on the table, flopped into his

seat, making himself comfortable. A wide smile spread up his cheeks

as he ripped open his bag of chips, only getting on Conrad's nerves

even more. Didn't the Art Club have meetings on Thursdays?

Fridays? Whatever. He just wanted the twerp gone.

"Hey, man," said Ethan, sticking his feet up on the bench across from himself.

Always being a quick eater, Conrad shoving the rest of his pizza in his mouth, already finished with his chips and juice then slinging his backpack over his shoulders after jumping up from his seat. He noticed Ethan and Timothy stayed seated as he made his way out onto the field, where a few kids either sat on the grass or played with a soccer ball they were kicking back and forth to each other.

Shoes stomping on the grass behind him nearly had him stop suddenly, whipping around and facing whoever was following him. But he already knew who it was. The scent of little twerp, which was mostly just washed clothes and hair gel, swarming all his senses.

Having had enough, impatience climbing to the sky, Conrad whirling around, not caring if he flung up some dirt in the process.

"Can't you just go away!?" he yelled at a following Gary, getting in his face. He would have pushed him in the shoulder but the other boy had already taken a few hurried steps back, arms crossing in front of himself. "Go! Get away from me!" Stretching his mouth until it was wide open, not caring who heard him, or if his voice traveled all the

way across the country or not, as long as the other boy understood

him word for word. Which he obviously didn't, arms now uncrossed

and eyes looking elsewhere, further past Conrad, to the very edge of

the field where a portion of the chain-linked fence blocked off the

waves from the ocean.

Slowly moving across the water, a vessel floated to Dock Thirty-

Five, only coming to a complete stop when it had lined up with the

wooden structure.

Conrad watched a couple of people disembark, wearing what looked

to be business attire, some in suits and keeping hands on top of their

hats to keep them from floating away into the wind. Others had on

long, black overcoats, cinching the sides of their jackets together as if

they were hiding something. Conrad turned his attention back to the

scared boy who had his hands clasped together, slowly shaking his

head. What was under the coats, he figured had to be weapons of

some kind, though why they would need them, he had no idea.

By the time Ethan and Timothy came out on the field, it seemed as if

most of the yard duty teachers had either sprinted to where the students entered the school off the boat, scrambling to the docks, or ordering all the kids out on the field to clear from the center of the lawn and make some space.

"What's going on?" asked Ethan, forehead wrinkling while Timothy's eyebrow made a mad dash upward. Conrad shrugged, head turning so he had Gary in his sight again, hands growing warm once he noticed the other boy was taking a few steps toward Ethan and Timothy so he could hide behind them. And who should come marching out of the cafeteria, eyes widening as if he were ready for an exciting day, was none other than Wyatt, straightening the tie he had on which matched his black suit.

"Everybody, out of the way! We have special guests." Wyatt waved his arms from side to side, shooing them all back. From the right side of the island, no longer coming up the dock, some of their visitors approaching the gate, and Wyatt speed walking to the structure so he could unlock it. As soon as he flung the gate open, Conrad's eyes first fell upon a woman he hoped never to see again. Her now strait, brown hair hanging down her shoulders, flicking it back with one hand and holding the other up in a greeting.

"There he is!" she cooed, pointing at someone. "It is such an honor to see you, young man. Placed in the wrong school, and on this old island to boot. Well, all that is going to change very quickly. Just make your way towards me and we'll get this all sorted out."

"No!" came the angry shout from Gary, staying in his spot behind Ethan and Timothy.

Mrs. Carlson placed her hands on her hips, her cheerful smile fading. A few of the people in long overcoats stepped forward, looking as if they were going to make an arrest. Conrad didn't understand it. Why would they just now come for him? Bertram acted like he never knew where he was in the first place.

"I'm sorry, honey." Mrs. Carlson began motioning for one of the men in the overcoats to continue moving forward. "Your uncle has requested your presence. I'm afraid you *have* to see him."

"This doesn't make sense. He should be allowed to stay here. It's his choice." Ethan stepped forward, hands clutched into tight fists, the beginnings of a snarl on his face.

"Excuse me?" said Mrs. Carlson, smoothing her hair with both hands, then flicking it over her shoulder. "This is not his or *your* decision to make. Come on now, Gary. It is time to go-"

"Utterly ridiculous," said Timothy, loud enough for Mrs. Carlson to hear him.

"Gary." She stomped a high-heeled pump. "*It's time to go.*"

In what Conrad thought to be an act of desperation, Gary grabbed the sleeve of Timothy's shirt, wrinkling the fabric, almost tugging the other boy to the ground.

"Hey!" growled Timothy, teeth bared. "Don't drag Locke into this." He whipped his arm back to himself, smoothing the fabric afterward. "Okay, now pay attention," Timothy instructed in a quieter tone of voice. "Whatever you do, don't panic. Locke will see you again next year at the school for the Gifted. He promises."

But Gary couldn't be convinced, moving his arm out of the way so the man in the overcoat couldn't grab it. But he merely hoisted Gary in the air, hauling the struggling boy to Mrs. Carlson. As Conrad watched Gary being carried away, yelling and fighting as he went, he couldn't help but feel bad for wishing the dang boy to leave and never come back. At least, that was what he'd originally thought. Now, he couldn't help but feel sorry for him, especially with Ethan and

Timothy's faces scrunched up in anger. They just had to make every-thing ten times worse, didn't they?

A weird, prickly sensation attacked Conrad's cheek. He then real-ized the entire field of kids had stopped what they were doing to stare at them.

"What now?" asked some boy Conrad never met before, standing rigidly with his arms by his sides. "What's going to happen now that the Swift boy is gone?"

"Who cares!?" shouted someone else Conrad couldn't see. "He didn't belong here, anyway."

"He went to this school along with everyone else, didn't he?" said someone Conrad didn't expect to be sticking up for Gary. "So, yeah," continued Darren. "I'd say he belonged here." Before he could even comprehend what was going on, the entire field of kids burst into loud chatter, either arguing about what good it was for them to have the lit-tle brat gone or how they felt sorry about him leaving.

"Alright, everybody! That's enough,' shouted a yard duty teacher. "Please go back to your former activities." Right after she spoke, the bell signaling the end of lunchtime rang, shrieking in their ears.

Conrad managed to ignore the groans floating through the air of disgruntled kids not ready to return to class. The only thought running through his mind was one of resentment and regret. He may not have liked the scrawny pest but that didn't mean he wanted to see him dragged off like a stray dog being taken to the pound.

He had other things to worry about, anyway. Like the fact his time to leave approached quickly, the cool air making sure he didn't forget it.

Chapter 13: The First Kiss

As their last class of the day ended, Conrad didn't even bother neatly putting his school work into his backpack, shoving his binder and textbook inside, throwing it on his back without even zipping it back up.

"See you inside." He nodded at Timothy and Ethan as they exited out of the class, on their way to the dorms. He waited for Beverly to make her way by him, the smell of her floral perfume wafting up his nose. Conrad waited until they were outside the building to take her by the hand, pushing her softly against the classroom wall.

"Hmm…wasn't expecting that." Beverly swiped hair off her shoulder, shrugging.

"Neither was I, but…I don't know of any other way of telling you this." Conrad raised both of his hands, staring at the girl he had conversations with ever since they came off the boat. Beverly cocked her head to the side, eyebrows raised as she waited. "Tomorrow, I'm not going to be myself. It's going to get me kicked out of school-But just know it's not the real me-right? I guess what I'm trying to say-"

"Boy, I know the real you." Beverly put a finger over his lips, silencing him. "Just go on and do what you gotta do. I'll be waiting for you." And before he knew what was going to happen, Beverly leaned in real close, exhaled slowly out her nose then tugged him forward so she could kiss him on the lips. She leaned back for a second, breathing in, studying Conrad's facial expression, and he had no idea what he looked like. Probably a clueless numbskull.

He couldn't let it all end this way. This time, Conrad was the one who put his lips on hers, not minding Beverly wrapping her arms around the back of his neck, pulling him closer.

If Conrad had to tell anybody how he felt in the moment, he'd leave out the part where his heart pounded in his chest, not willing to admit to anybody what a big blob of nerves he was. But in a split second, all the fear began to drain away, to melt into nothingness. He had a hard time believing how he could be so lucky, the stars rearranging so he couldn't possibly be sad, or angry, or fed up. Everything was exactly as it should be. Until-

"Hey! Students should not be out here! Go to your next class before you both get sent to the principal's office."

He sighed in aggravation, taking Beverly's hand and walking away from the older woman who squinted at them as if she had a hard time seeing. Conrad would recommend she put her glasses back on. Sure, they were old and ugly, the frames around the glass peeling off the surface, but she'd have an easier time seeing who she was yelling at.

The roofs of the dorms appeared, the flickering lights from the windows calling to them. Conrad wished he could take Beverly away from the rooms where they could be alone. Maybe out in the woods, far away from everyone else. Yeah, right. They'd be caught in a second by a stupid yard duty teacher.

"Even though your leaving," said Beverly, swinging their hands as they walked. "I'm still looking forward to tomorrow."

Conrad didn't ask why, simply glancing at her and raising his eyebrows. Beverly shrugged, a slight smile on her face. "Oh, you know, your brother and Nova."

It felt like he rolled his eyes one hundred times in a single year, but he didn't resist doing it again. He already knew he was going to have a long day.

Chapter 14: Taking Down the Pyroglee

The coming of lunch time the next day jumpstarted his nerves, tempting butterflies in his stomach to fly around in a mad dash. He hardly paid attention to mind numbing math problems or boring stories their English teacher read to them on a daily basis. All he knew was he had to leave. NOW.

Okay, not immediately, but any time soon would be great.

The ringing of the bell was like a heavenly noise to him. He all but jumped out of his seat, grabbing his backpack, speed-walking to the door, not caring if Ethan and Timothy kept up.

"So, uh, are we running sprints today?" He could hear Timothy ask casually to Ethan, both of them keeping behind him.

"Man, I don't know," responded Ethan, trying to sound irritated, but Conrad could hear the nerves in his voice. "They got us running miles for no reason." As soon as he reached the door, Timothy sped past him, arm brushing against his. Conrad wanted to shout vulgar words at the taller boy, who didn't look at him once. He kept going straight forward, only stopping when coming next to a building which held most of the math and science classes.

Swiping her long hair behind her back, Nova Bringham clutching her binders under one arm while holding a notebook in her hand. A grin began climbing up her face once she spotted Timothy, picking up her feet so she could stand next to him. He wasn't surprised when she grabbed him by the hand, leaning in really close to him. *I mean, why be surprised anymore?*

Conrad threw up his hands, wondering why he stood all alone out on the field.

"Oh, my God," said a girl walking with her friend. "Nova and

Timothy. Together. When did this happen?"

"I don't know," said her friend, flipping brunette hair over her shoulder. "But I heard she has, like, three boyfriends already. She probably broke up with them or something."

"Ew. And now she's with Timothy. Gross."

As much as he wanted to agree with her, Conrad kept his mouth closed. He raised his hand, waving it so it flopped from side to side.

Timothy jerked his head around so he looked straight at Conrad. A frown fell on his face, and he quickly turned to Nova, hand no longer interlocked with hers but gesticulating wildly.

Nova crossed her arms then motioned for him to go, which he abruptly did, in his little prance.

"What now?" asked Ethan when Timothy made a stop right in front of them. Conrad simply pointed at the dorms, moving his legs up and down on the way to their rooms, Ethan and Timothy trying to keep up.

"You guys ready?" Conrad shook out his arms, hefting his backpack up so it sat higher on his shoulders.

"Uh, what are we supposed to do again?" Timothy began scratching the back of his head, perplexed.

"I thought I told you guys this-"

"Just do what I'm doing, man," Ethan interrupted, staring Timothy in the face while pointing at his eyes with two fingers. Ethan put a foot forward, resting a hand on his knee as if about to start running. Timothy did the same, confusion floating in his eyes. "Okay, on the count of three. One…Two…Three!"

In a burst of energy, Ethan ran to the center of the field, stopping suddenly and pointing behind himself.

"He's going crazy! Everybody, watch out!"

And a few seconds later, finally remembering what to do, Timothy also ran from his spot, shouting, "He's shooting flames at us! Run!"

Stretching his arms out, breathing in some fresh air, Conrad placed one foot behind himself before blasting off, hands heating up along the way.

Shoving his hands in the air, fingers wriggling, watching as a long line of dangerous hot flames shot up to the sky. All he got was a couple of curious looks, so he decided to change things to a more hostile level. Instead of reaching up, he shot his hands forward, releasing another blast of scorching hot flames, fire aimed at the fence sur-

rounding the school. While part of it began to crumple to the ground,

he could hear a few panicked screams, along with the whistles of

some yard duty teachers. But that wasn't enough.

Conrad stomped his foot, let out what he thought to be a fierce yell,

then hurled flames into more of the fence, sending it flying into the

ocean. The whistles became more fervent, piercing in his ears.

"Hey, what are you doing?!" shouted someone who he assumed to

be Wyatt. Conrad knew all he had to do was show the man his red-

dening eyes, which he promptly did, and he'd quickly move out of the

way. Wyatt took several steps back, calling for more yard duty teach-

ers to come stop the dangerous pyroglee student.

"Come quickly!" he yelled, waving his arms. "He's destroying the

field!" Just like that, yard duty teachers formed a half circle around

him, forcing Conrad to aim upwards again. Well, since they wanted to

block him… He jumped into the air, slamming both feet down once

his shoes made contact with the ground, blasting fire through a gap

between two-yard duty teachers. Letting out panicking cries before

jumping out of the way, one of them swatting at the air as if the tips of their fingers had felt the flames.

Everything was going exactly as it should. Then he felt it. A quick blow to the back of his head. He fell to his knees before tumbling on his side, seeing a long stick fall to the ground beside him. Conrad rolled onto his back just as Ms. Violet peered down at him, mouth open in shock.

All he could remember afterwards was a blanket of pitch black clouds blocking his entire vision.

…

He urged himself to wake up inside his head, not really sure how long he'd been in bed. He wasn't even sure which bed he was in. The one at Buzzard or his own at Liz's house. All Conrad knew, was he had to get out and fast.

Conrad did his best to sit up, but was instantly held back by straps on his chest pinning him to the mattress. Not just his chest but arms too. He tried to kick his foot up, only to find out his legs were strapped to the bed as well.

If the situation had been any different, he'd have been a ball of fiery rage, fighting to get the straps off himself, yelling at whichever jerks ran the establishment to release him or he'd tear the whole place apart using his bare hands.

Instead, he rested his head back on the thin pillow, noticing his covers were stark white with a blue trim.

Although the blankets hid the tight straps on his arms and legs, he knew without a doubt he wasn't escaping any time soon. The drowsiness he was going through made sure of that.

Two framed paintings of grassy woodlands hung on both walls beside him, while a long wooden door with a bronze knob extended to the floor. Conrad peeked up at the wall in front of him, eyeing the long, glass partition going across it. He was being watched.

He swung his head to the side, keeping his eyes on the door which was his only way out. As soon as he did, a searing pain came over the back of his head, digging into his skull, prompting him to clench his eyes shut again. Before he could groan in pain, regretting his life decisions in the process, two quick knocks on the door got his attention. Without even thinking about it, beginning to sink under the covers, eyes shutting in the process.

The tapping of shoes on the floor rang in his ears, along with the sound of voices speaking quietly to each other.

"What's going to happen to him, now?" asked someone Conrad could only assume to be a new worker.

"Refuse," said someone else with a grouch in his voice. "We'll get him in the van then head on back inside. It'll be the last we'll ever see of him."

Conrad hears a 'Pop!', realizing they just opened something. He grits his teeth, braces himself, waiting for the sharp pain which was sure to ensue.

Conrad thought if he had to grit his teeth anymore, they'd be nothing but a pile of dust, but as soon as the needle pieced his skin, he couldn't help but clamp his teeth together once again. It seemed like no matter how long he kept his eyes squeezed shut, the pain would never go away. He was in a constant state of a burning pain. Not just coming from the needle they stuck him with, but the flow of the burning medicine through his veins.

He didn't know what kind of sleep concoction could make someone's insides feel as if they'd been dumped in a boiling river filled with flesh eating piranhas, but the urge to cry out in pain nearly over-took him, but not as quickly as the sensation of wanting to fall asleep. He promptly did so, not caring where'd he'd wake up this time. Just as long as the pain went away.

The rumbling of the floor underneath him, his hands tied together with a fabric he thought to be rope, and the sound of cars zooming on a road. He wracked his mind trying to remember where they could possibly be headed to, when one word suddenly entered his mind. Re-fuse.

Chapter 15: All Aboard

Building after building raced by the window next to him, making

Conrad realize the further they went, the farther away from the Red-

wood Forest they were getting. And he couldn't let the car go on for

that long. No, not happening.

Taking a deep breath, Conrad lifted his legs, curled them to himself

then flung them out so they smashed into the back of the driver seat.

The driver swung the wheel to the left, making the car swerve so it

nearly hit another vehicle. The second car, which happened to be a black jeep, swerved out of the way, avoiding a near collision.

Far from finished, Conrad brought his legs back again before ramming them into the back of the driver's seat.

"Hey!" the middle aged man yelled, face dripping sweat. Hmm, he was making him nervous. Good. Encouraged, he rammed his feet into the front seat one last time, hard enough to make the driver swivel the car so it was speeding off the freeway. Their car sped onto a crowded street, the honking of horns filling the air.

"Can't you people see I'm dealing with a crazy-" Before he could finish his sentence, Conrad thrust his hands forward until they were gripping the back of the man's collar. The man yelled out in a panic before swinging the car next to a sidewalk and stomping on the break.

Little did the man know, this was exactly what Conrad wanted him to do.

Speaking so he had a growl to his voice, Conrad demanded, "Let me out of the car."

The driver let out a mix between a nervous laugh and an unbelieving one before saying, "No can do. Not going to happen in this lifetime or the next." *Fine.*

In a fit of annoyance, Conrad swung his arms back as best as he could before smashing them into the window right next to him, happy to see the glass about to shatter from the force of the blows. But, to Conrad's annoyance, the car merely pulled away from the sidewalk, turning to where most of the other cars headed to a street light.

"Let me out," snapped Conrad, "Or I'll set this whole car on fire." The driver looked behind himself at Conrad for a quick second, forehead beginning to wrinkle. "The flames don't bother me...but I'm not so sure about you."

Finally, the car came to an abrupt stop in the middle of the road, prompting more car horns to blast through the air.

The driver swiveled around, eyebrows raised, mouth open as if he just saw a monster with sharp teeth outside the window. The locks on the door clicked, the urge to rush out onto the street taking over his mind. There was only one problem.

Beyond frustrated, Conrad stuck his tied together hands forward, eyebrows raised. The driver sighed, unbuckled his seatbelt then leaned toward Conrad so he could untie the rope from around his wrists. He shook his hands once they were free, hoping to wake them

108

from the sleep they'd fallen into.

Without wasting any time, Conrad pushed his door open, a cool breeze ruffling his hair. He slammed the door shut without looking back, keeping his vision locked straight ahead.

To his relief, most of the townspeople went back to their daily routines, walking inside the shops or chatting with friends.

Hoisting his bag higher up on his shoulders, Conrad made his way around multiple pedestrians, some in sweatpants and sweaters while others breezed by in simple tees and shorts, not minding the cold. But he, on the other hand, did mind. He pulled the hood to his sweater over his head, pulling out his sleeves afterward, making it known the breeze wasn't invited anywhere near him.

To his left, Conrad saw the sign which told him he was exactly where he was supposed to be. It flopped in the wind as if it were waving to someone. Cove Train Station. He began walking to the sunflower yellow sign, hands stuffed into the pockets on his sweater.

"Cove Train Station!" yelled a man in a beige suit, a stop sign red sweater underneath. "All who want to board come this way!"

By this time, a crowd of people started assembling past the sign,

Conrad picking up his feet to follow. The man waving everyone along, handing out pamphlets, COVE CITY EXPRESS being the title, cast Conrad a suspicious look, most likely wondering where his parents were at.

All of a sudden, a boy about his age bumped into him, not caring in the slightest who he knocked over. Conrad opened his mouth to tell him off, fully prepared to shout at him, but, the other boy cut him off to say, "You're going to the Redwood Forest, too, huh? You doing this for a school project or something?"

Conrad merely shook his head, not in the mood for a long conversation, or any type of conversation for that matter. "The Redwood Forest," the talkative boy continued, like he was determined to socialize. "I heard some weird stuff about this place. Heard this is where Deputy and Silence disappeared. Them and their two henchmen. What were their names again?"

"Johnny and Cosmo," Conrad said as they neared the entrance to the forest. The tall redwoods made themselves known, towering above all of them, the tips of their trunks appearing to scrape the sky.

"Oh, yeah! Weren't they part of some gang or something?" Conrad did his best to not roll his eyes, giving a small shrug, instead.

To their right, a dirt trail leading into the forest caught his attention, dipping between the redwoods, giving Conrad the heads up they were almost to the train station.

Without wasting any time, they began walking on the path which would lead them to their destination, strolling to what was supposed to be a relaxing and beautiful sight seeing jaunt through the forest. But Conrad couldn't rid what he was about to do from his mind.

"What's wrong, boy?" He heard his father say in his mind. "You getting nervous on me? Johnny, come here." Conrad would stand with his hands clasped together as his uncle stood next to his father with arms crossed. "You tell this weasel how we don't let fear get the best of us. How we simply get the job done." After his father left, his uncle Johnny would squat down, one hand on his knee then state, "What do I always tell you? Sometimes you just gotta go. Put your foot on the gas, and go as fast as you can. No hesitation."

Conrad shook his head, trying to clear his mind from wandering thoughts. At the same time, they came near a cabin which was painted lime green, standing taller than it was wide. Conrad thought a drawing of a face with its tongue sticking out at them would have went well with the obnoxious, bright building.

In front of it, sticking out of the dirt, was the train tracks, dark bronze in color so the sunlight had a glow running along its surface. The train itself was nowhere to be seen, reminding Conrad he had to wait a few more dang minutes before he actually started his journey further into the forest.

All of a sudden, the same boy who'd been talking to him earlier came by his side again, and Conrad's arms and shoulders tightened, wondering what it would take to get rid of the nuisance who wouldn't leave him alone.

"My name is Jake, by the way." He ran a hand through his pecan brown hair, light, dirt brown, eyes focused on him. Because that's the way Conrad saw him. As dirt. "I just wanted to see what this place is like. What about you?"

Conrad shrugged, not bothering to look at the other boy.

"Oh…then what's *your* name?" *None of your freakin' business,* Conrad wanted to grouch out loud but simply sped up instead, heading to the white chairs in front of the tracks. He whipped a chair around as soon as he came by the tracks and made sure to flop into it, ignoring Jake as he passed by him with a hurt look on his face, casting Conrad one last look before heading to a seat further to the right.

"Everybody, hurry up and find your seats!" The man who Conrad now assumed to be the train conductor waved his arms, meaning for them to come forward. In a manner of seconds, Conrad heard the sound of the train coming down the tracks, whirring as it blew out steam.

People began rummaging in their pockets for their boarding passes, reminding Conrad he should be doing the same. Once he found the scrunched up paper in his pocket, he set it on his lap, soon watching as the train slowed to a stop. Conrad leaned back in his seat, the memory of his dad meeting Johnny and Cosmo for the first time, both of his uncles, racing inside his mind.

Chapter 16: The Caplin Brothers

According to Johnny, he had met Deputy before he was with Silence, out on the streets where he had gone to get some air. The Caplin Gang, which he had been a part of, hadn't taken too kindly to Cosmo's 'smart mouth', and set up a plan to have him arrested. Not only was he arrested, but placed in an insane asylum on the West side of New Jersey.

"We were already going through a hard time," explained Johnny, kicking back in his seat, legs rested on another chair in front of him. "Cosmo's wife killed by somebody else in another gang, and now this. Nothing seemed to be going the way it was supposed to. Cosmo in this nut house, the gang setting the whole thing up, and then I hear this voice calling to me. I don't recognize it at first, but then I realize it sounds just like the guy from all these news channels, talking about this criminal named Deputy, who came from the south, and disappeared just like that.

So, yeah, I get to know him, and find out he really is the guy who all these newscasters are talking about. He tells me he's got these inside sources who tell him everything, and was trying to recruit people for his own gang.

At first, I thought, *this guy is crazy,* and didn't want anything to do with him. But then he mentioned knowing about Cosmo, said he could help get him out." Johnny paused, eyes directed at the ceiling to the motel they'd stopped at.

Twiddling his fingers, he soon continued, "I didn't see anything else I could do but follow him and leave the Caplin Gang for good." He smirked then nudged Conrad in the arm.

"So, anyway, we plan to get into the facility for the mentally unstable. Your father manages to get me a doctor's suit, making it look like I worked there and everything. And let me tell you, kid, this place had four floors and dim lights, making it seem like you were in a haunted mansion.

When I found out Cosmo was on the second floor, in the room number they gave me, I walked to the right door, pen and notebook in hand. I knock on his door and say, "Hey, hey," In a low voice. And when he doesn't answer, I'm like, "*Moron*. It's me. Grab your stuff cause' we're getting out of here."

Conrad scratched his head, trying to visualize the whole thing. The mental hospital, doctors roaming the hallways, and hardly being able to see anything. Hmm. It sounded like a fun maze to him.

"By the time I enter the room, I see Cosmo in a white jumpsuit, sitting on the bed, looking all irritated and junk. I simply pull him up by the arm and say, "*Come on,* you dope. We're getting out of here."

"We're walking down the hall, and Cosmo begins trying to tug his arm away from me."

"What are you doing?" I mean, by this point, I'm ready to throw him back into his little room. If he gets tested on, he gets tested on. See if I care."

"I just want them to think I'm struggling," he answered back at me.

"I get it, and by the time we make it outside, Deputy pulled up in a van next to us. He tells us to get in when an alarm goes off on the building. I hurry up and tell him, "Believe me, boss, I'm a monster behind the wheel." He doesn't even question it. Just hops out and gets in the back seat, leaving me to do my thing."

"Did you guys end up escaping?" Conrad had asked, mouth wide open.

"Well, if we didn't, you wouldn't be sitting here now, would ya'?" Conrad let out a snicker, before another question popped into his mind.

"Could you teach me how to drive one day, Uncle Johnny?"

"Sure thing, little man. We can even get started right away if you're up for it. All we have to do is tie some weight under your shoes and we can get started. I hear the dessert up here is a good place to burn some rubber."

It didn't matter he was only ten years old at the time, or barely knew a thing about driving, but, *man*, his uncle Johnny was going to teach him and he couldn't ask for anything more. Adrenaline racing, heat pounding against his chest, the daunting task of attempting to release his parents from the Disappearing Hole now felt like it was going to be a walk in the park. That is, if he didn't face any of the crime boss's henchmen on the way there.

Chapter 17: Offered Assistance

He was one of the first ones to jump out of his seat, butterflies swirl-

ing around in his stomach, the ability to swallow now hard work.

  A worker from up top began spinning a wheel which let down the

steps they had to climb to reach the top. He promptly began his way

to the stairs, putting his clammy hands on the railings to steady him-

self. He didn't want to be the idiot who lost his balance and fell to the

bottom. Once he came to the top, he went to the very back where

there were just three seats. He plopped down on the soft cushion, feeling relief swarm through him when he put his head back against the top part of the seat.

Conrad chose to ignore most of the passengers settling down, chatting excitingly with each other. Mostly the little kids, running to the sides of the train so they could get a good look at the scenery, only to be chastised by their parents who warned them to sit back in their seats. Did they want to be flung off into the woods? No, they didn't think so.

Once everybody was in their seats, the train conductor began waving his arms above his head, signaling it was time for them to take off. As soon as the train's engines began to whirr, a couple of people let out cheers, white smoke drifting into the air.

"What did I tell you about playing with your Gift, boy?" He heard his mother's voice come from out of nowhere. And suddenly, he was five years old again, making fire come out of his hands. "Be careful with it. I know it's a part of who we are, but it can also get out of control. They're not kidding when they talk about those dangerous fire types on the news. Believe me."

"But dad say's-" he'd protest before being sharply cut off.

"I know. I know." She'd wave her hands in front of her face and shake her head, eyes narrowed. "But listen to *me*, be careful with you Gift. I know he's okay with you releasing all that energy, but you could hurt someone, or even worse, hurt yourself. So, keep it away." Conrad blew out a puff of air, rubbing his hands together. The first stop would be what he was looking for. Where he needed to be. All he had to do was wait and be patient. All he had to do-

"So, I was thinking," said no one other than Jake, plopping down next to him. Conrad flung his head back in irritation, hands landing on his face, covering his eyes. "We got twenty-minutes until this thing's over. And all we see are these humongous trees. When do we stop and get something to eat, you know?"

If Conrad knew the answer to his question, he'd probably tell him, but the only thing he could see himself doing was flinging Jake over the rails then sitting comfortably back into his seat like nothing happened. Yeah, that would be nice. *Crap!* He roughly shook his head, trying to rid his mind of seriously hurting the other boy by flinging him off the train, onto the waiting tracks below.

To his relief, Jake immediately shut his mouth, bringing Conrad the relief he drastically needed. The only thing was, the tiny hairs on his face stood straight up, letting him know he was being stared at.

"Hey…" Began Jake hesitantly, an uneasiness to his voice. "Are you okay?"

"Just leave me alone," Conrad said with a growl, not knowing any other way he could make himself clearer. Except… Widening his eyes, Conrad finally flung his hands off them, making sure Jake was in his line of site.

The other boy let out a gasp, leaning back in his seat as if to ward off any attack from the angry boy seated next to him. The astonishment didn't last long, turning into curiosity as he said, "Woah, are you one of those fire types? Can you make fire come out of your hands? 'Cause that would be so cool." The rolling of the wheels began to slow, alerting Conrad they were almost to the first stop. He felt himself scoot closer to the edge of his seat, nearly dying from anticipation.

The wheels went over two bumps before coming to a complete stop, the smell of maple wafting up his nostrils.

"Okay, everyone," commanded the train conductor. "We have

reached our first destination. Please exit from the side of the car and remember to watch your steps. Don't want anyone tumbling to the ground.

Conrad immediately got to his feet, noticing Jake getting up as well. He began to realize none of the adults searched for their son, all going to the stairs at the side of the car. It was then it hit him the other boy was all alone, probably catching the first train he could get a ticket to.

"You always come to these by yourself?" He couldn't help but glance at the other boy, suddenly curious.

"Eh, sometimes, when I got nothing better to do. This will take your mind off things, you know?"

"Sure." Conrad pulled his sweater tighter around himself, keeping behind a family with about three little kids. They made their way down the steps, the train conductor stopping to speak to another worker. That was all he needed.

He didn't even think about it as he began shoving people out of his way, a woman pulling her kids behind her and yelling, "Watch where you're going!" Running down the steps was no problem for him, not even bothering to hold on to a rail. The only thing on his mind was

"Go!", so, he did nothing else but bolt between the first two Redwoods next to the train tracks, not focusing on anything else around
him, not even a sharp whistle blowing through the air. Conrad knew
he had been spotted. With his mind clearer, Conrad thought maybe he
should check to see if someone was with him. As soon as he slowed
to a speed walk, he saw there was indeed someone beside him. And
the urge to throw Jake onto the train tracks became even stronger.

Chapter 18: The Criminals Are Back

Before Conrad had a chance to say anything, he blew in a puff of air, trying to keep himself calm. Unfortunately, the outrage burst forth anyway, coming out as a tired shout he knew somebody could probably hear.

"Man, what are you doing?! Get back on the train!" Jake simply shrugged, managing to keep up with a steaming, eyes on the verge of turning blood red, Conrad.

"Look," said Jake, taking off his jacket and wrapping it around his

125

waist, "I know you're about to do something stupid. Just wanted to be here in case something goes wrong and you need help."

"You have no idea what you're doing." Conrad held the sides of his head with both hands, shaking it. "I mean, come on! You're going to get yourself killed."

"It's that bad? What are you about to do?"

"Don't worry about it." Conrad couldn't believe both of his uncles were coming out in him. "Just go on back to your seat. Pretend you never saw me."

The other boy didn't say anything else, still following Conrad, who was beginning to feel sorry for him. The moron thought he was doing him a favor, thought he could keep him out of trouble just like that. Well, if he had to see what was waiting for them, he would just have to deal with the consequences.

The walk through the Redwood Forest, or, in Conrad's case, speed-walk, went on and on, the sun going down behind the dark brown trees, leaving them in a shadowy, blank space Conrad had a hard time seeing through. Everything had gone quiet. Not even the birds were chirping anymore. The only thing he could hear was the 'crunch' '

'crunch' 'crunch' of his shoes. Well, *their* shoes. Conrad let out a be-yond irritated sigh. *Stupid idiot-* He let the thought be cutoff as the sound of voices could be heard in the distance. *Of, course...*

"Hey, look who it is." Several of Magnum's henchmen turned around, eyes on Conrad then focusing on Jake. He should've known. Magnum *would* send his lab rats out to where he was going, which happened to be several spaces behind them, dipping into the ground, a sheet of black inside it, making it appear to be a wide-open mouth.

"Well, well," said Vanish, the click of guns reaching Conrad's ears. "We couldn't be happier to see you. Why don't you come over here and take a seat?"

"I'm fine where I am." Conrad began to dig his foot into the ground, not looking to play any games. He then looked over at Jake, the boy watching the three men wielding the guns and back at Conrad, mouth opening into a small gape, fear radiating off him in waves.

"All we want from you is cooperation." Vanish nodded, probably expecting the boy to do everything he asked. "Go back to where you came from, and you'll never hear from us again. It's as simple as that." Conrad heard a shuffling of feet on his right, realizing Jake had stepped up so he was standing right beside him.

"And who is this?" Vanish let out a snide laugh, looking to the two other men as if the situation was too hilarious.

"No one." Conrad swiped his hand so it almost hit Jake in the face.

"Oh, really?" said Vanish, eyelids furrowed. "Seems to me like you brought some assistance."

"What? No!" Conrad exclaimed, nearly at his wits end. "He's just some random guy I met on the train. He's nothin'." Then it hit him. "And what the heck are you guys even doing here?"

"We were sent to stop you from completing your mission. And it looks like we came at the perfect time." Vanish held up his arm and moved his index finger forward and backward, meaning for one of the gunmen to step forward.

At this point, he knew the only way to accomplish what he came there to do was to use force, and if Magnum wanted some of his co-workers to perish for their cause then so be it. He would gladly help out with that.

Heat began its slow crawl into his hands, hoping his irises didn't give him away by changing into the threatening blood red color.

They'd be on to him in a second. He held his head down, closing his eyes in the process, counting down from *five*.

"What's he doing?" he heard someone laugh, who sounded like another new worker. *Four*.

"Hey, kid, are you alright? We making you wheezy?" More laughter. *Three*. He could hear Jake shuffling his feet on the ground, growing more and more nervous. Conrad could just imagine the sweat sliding down his face. *Two*.

"And where's that book at? You still haven't told us what you've done with it." *One*.

In one swift move, Conrad was able to shove Jake out of the way of the gunmen, causing him to stumble before falling to the ground. Knowing Magnum's workers would be quick to ready themselves for battle, he gathered his Gift, summoning the raw power, his hands heating up until they felt like they had become their own burning fire.

He directed his attention to the man closest to him, His Gift sizzling, ready to be unleashed. And just like that, fire engulphed his entire body, whirling around and around in a circle, his cries of pain reaching far and wide. Conrad could imagine to the edge of the forest. But he had no time to think about it, grabbing onto a gun so the nozzle was next to his head instead of right in front of it.

Two bullets fired out of it, and Jake's yell of terror went into Conrad's ears, reminding him he didn't come alone. Yet again... He went past another man, sliding past him so he could rush up on Vanish, grabbing him by both of his arms and yanking the panicking man in front of him, shielding himself from view. If it had to be any time, it had to be now.

Conrad began by stomping his foot once on the ground then crying out, "Emergo, NOW!" They may not have been the magical words Mr. Grey said they were, but, hey, they worked.

A rumbling of the ground nearly shook Conrad off his feet, along with the gunmen who now only held their weapons with one hand, using the other to try and steady themselves. If he peered around Vanish, he could see some of the men struggling to keep their balance, or Jake, who had thrown himself onto the ground, hands covering his head.

A bright flash of light. The rumbling of the ground intensifying. Cries of terror breaking out.

130

He slowly made his way out from behind Vanish once the shaking had ceased, noticing five new adults were now standing in front of him, with their backs in his line of site.

Chapter 19: Goodbye, Jake?

Conrad didn't know what to do with himself. Run in excitement? Let out an earth-shattering shout? Anything had to be better than just standing there, completing nothing at all. Even the men behind him seemed to be at a complete loss, arms hanging by their sides, mouths hanging open in shock.

All he knew was he better get out the way. And fast. Conrad spotted an old Redwood to his right, almost right next to him.

He began sliding his shoes across the ground, trying not to make a sound, but as soon as he could hear the snap of a twig underneath his feet, he made a mad dash behind the tree, sliding to his knees, not looking forward to the blood bath which was sure to occur.

The first gunshot went off, ringing through the air, and the next 'pop!' of the bullets burst through his ears, making him throw his hands over them. He could only hope Magnum's men were the only ones who took the injuries from the gunshots

"I think that's all of them."

Conrad peeked around the tree at the sound of the familiar, gruff, voice, keeping low so as not to attract any attention. Two men who looked similar, wearing black suits, and who had their hair slicked back, had their fingers clutching automatic rifles. Another man stood between them, muscles like hills on his arms, holding a pistol.

"Deputy...who where they?" A woman's voice, soft with a little bit of country to it.

"Don't know, but I have a feeling we're about to find out...Okay, I'll give you three seconds to come out from over there. One.." Without thinking about it, Conrad jumped to his feet, having a hard time believing what was happening. He quickly came out from behind the tree but stood completely still when he was in their line of site.

For several minutes, they stood in their same spots, staring at each other, Conrad's heart pounding at what seemed to be one-hundred miles per hour.

A gasp suddenly went through the air, coming from a woman in a black jumpsuit with long black hair, and round eyes fading from blood red to a dark brown. Her hands began to rise to her mouth, eyes growing bigger.

Her eyes went to Deputy for a quick second before landing on Conrad again, the shock radiating all around her, causing her to hop in the air once before rushing to Conrad, arms wide open.

Like most situations forcing him to show affection, he simply froze as his mom threw her arms around him. But like someone pushing a start button sitting on his brain, he was finally able to open his own arms and return the hug, if not slowly, taking his time.

He still couldn't believe this was real.

Before saying anything, Jodie put her hands to her mouth, eyes widening as she observed her son, seemingly as shocked as Conrad.

"Look how tall he is, now." She pointed two fingers at him, a big smile on her face.

"Wow," mulled his Uncle Cosmo, fingering his chin. "How much time has gone by?"

"He was eleven when we left," snapped his Uncle Johnny. "He looks to be a teen now. How many years do you *think* passed by?"

"Okay, you know what?-" snarled Cosmo before being cut off.

"Age makes no difference," said Deputy in harsh tone of voice, re-minding Conrad of when he was being yelled at for not completing a task. "I just want to know if you're ready."

All he could think of to do was nod, hands by his side, before say-ing, "Yes, sir."

"Alright, then." Deputy stepped forward, belt wrapped around his floppy pants, and wearing a long overcoat over a white tank top, his rustic brown hair ruffling in the wind, while his jacket was swaying. "We'll head off into the city, first, get more supplies. Then go to the lair of that dumb crime boss. I have a bone to pick with him. Pointing your guns at me and my wife is one thing, but involving my son…" Deputy shook his head, eyes narrowing. "Now you're just asking for it." A tiny smile broke loose on Conrad's face before disappearing just as quickly, enjoying his dad's anger at the man who held him,

Ethan, and Timothy, hostage inside his lair.

He could remember the stupid tasks they completed for him, how

they took out criminals he thought were merely in his way. Criminals

he didn't want to be in competition with, who he thought were merely

lowlife scum. If he had the ability, Conrad would block Hypno from

out of his head or turn him against Magnum so they'd never bother

him again.

The sound of shoes running on the dirt, the click of a gun, and a

'BAM!' as the pistol went off. Conrad couldn't help but watch as

Jake fell onto the ground, dust floating up from where he hit the dirt.

Conrad's eyes widening at the site, lower lip dropping open in shock,

not looking forward to seeing blood pour out of the foolish boy he

met at the train station.

Chapter 20: Hello, Victoria

"You just…" Conrad grabbed at his hair with one hand, clinching the strands as if he meant to rip them out.

"Sorry," said Cosmo, appearing sheepish and lowering his gun, the left side of his lower lip dropping. "It's just sort of an instinct, you know?"

"No." Johnny shook his head, rolling his eyes. "You had no reason to shoot at him, plus your shot's getting rusty."

"At least I have a better aim than *you*-" Cosmo's hands went on his waist as he cast a glare at his brother, but his attention went elsewhere when a shuffling in the dirt where Jake fell down reached their ears.

To Conrad's surprise, and utter relief, Jake lifted himself off the ground, not even bothering to wipe the flecks of dirt off his shirt and pants, simply letting it fly off of him in the wind. His Uncle Cosmo's eyes narrowed as he must have realized his aim was, indeed, off.

Jake took an unsure step forward as if he was planning to run off again, but was instantly blocked by Deputy, who wore a frown on his face.

"Now, you listen to me, kid" he said in his gruff, country accent. "You tell no one about this, understood?" Jake flopped his head up and down, eyes bulging out of his head in shock as he observed the criminal brought out of the Disappearing Hole. "Then go on to your home, and don't come back out." Jake cast one last sympathetic look at Conrad before dashing back to the train station like his life depended on it.

"He's going to come out of his home sooner or later, boss," said Cosmo, scratching at the back of his head.

Deputy let out a snicker, casting Johnny an amused look. "Ah, I was just messing with him. He can come outside whenever he wants to. Can even blab about it to his friends if he feels like it."

Kicking a rock on the ground so it slid on the dirt underneath his shoe, Conrad's attention soon fell on a woman who made herself comfortable on the ground, arms laying on her legs, staring at nothing but the forest in front of her. She flung up her hand, feeling the top of her head, fingers going through her dark hair. And that's when the realization hit Conrad. Her dark skin tone, the sunflower hat she had worn when she jumped into the hole after everyone else…Victoria.

Not wanting to startle her, Conrad slowly made his way towards the confused woman, who had on a beige vest over a dark green top and capri pants. He slowly sat down next to her, trying to be discreet. Victoria whipped her head at him in shock, anyway, her mouth hanging open, staring at Conrad as if he had to be a ghost.

"Victoria…" he said, uncertain on how to word the next sentence. She looked over at him in surprise, intensely staring at his face. She made sure to lean closer to him so she could stare deep into his eyes, causing a drop of discomfort to rise in Conrad. He managed to subdue it, not scooting away like he wanted to.

"Little boy?" She ran a hand down the side of Conrad's face, and he quickly shut his eyes, only used to this amount of contact when he was much younger. He also made sure to nod his head, putting more assurance in her.

"I-I know your nephew. Ethan. He's my brother, now." Her eyes began to open wider, putting hands on her cheeks.

"How did y'all even find each other? When? How on earth did this happen?"

"Warren," he said briskly, rubbing his hands together. "We go to one of the schools he built." A proud smile broke out on her face, eyes lighting up. "Uh, not the good one," he added, scratching at the side of his arm.

"What do you mean by that?" He could tell by the sudden, hard anger in her voice he'd have to explain the whole thing, including the details regarding Warren, himself. So, Conrad promptly delve into the story, starting with how they first met at the obstacle course, how they went to the school for the Neglected Gifted, battled Poison's rogues, being trapped at Magnum's lair, and ending up at where he was at now.

Victoria didn't say anything, simply studying him, looking over his facial features. Conrad knew she was trying to let everything sink in, so he went quiet for a couple of seconds, not wanting to let all the information become too much.

"You know, Ethan." A slight laugh escaped from her throat. A tear promptly slid down her cheek next, making Conrad roll his eyes, only spurring on more laughter.

"Boy, don't be rolling your eyes at me." She nudged him on his arm, a smile stretching the corners of her cheeks.

"Alright, we're ready to head off," came Deputy's loud voice, clapping his hands twice. "Conrad, lead the way."

Jumping up from his seat, Conrad took one look at their whereabouts, spotted the trail he traveled on, and began walking down it like he knew the forest like his own name. The footsteps of everyone following after him was a reminder he did, indeed, accomplish one of his missions, and he couldn't stop the smile from spreading across his face. The only thing was, they were going back to the crime boss's lair. He could only imagine what could possibly happen if he saw his parents plus Johnny and Cosmo again. Not to mention the fact they gunned down some of his men.

Once they reached the edge of the woods, the sun beginning to disappear behind the horizon, Conrad couldn't help but notice the empty parking lot, all the tourists having had gone back home.

The parking lot lay directly ahead of them, Conrad's eyes on the car he drove to the forest. He put his hand in his pocket, feeling around for the car keys, and once he finally pulled them out, put his thumb on the button to unlock the door.

Opening the door to the driver's seat, Conrad got ready to enter, until he felt a firm grip on his shoulder.

"Hey, kid," said Johnny, grinning. "I know I taught you a few things, but how 'bout you leave the driving to the professionals?" As much as Conrad wanted to protest, he moved to the side, not foolish enough to think he could drive better than his uncle.

"What about another car?" said Cosmo, throwing up his hands. "We can't all fit in there." Instead of answering, Conrad lifted up a finger above his head, hoping they would get the point and fall silent. Luckily, they immediately did, and what Conrad considered an even better occurrence was when the black truck he rented drove into the parking lot. Right on time.

The driver of the vehicle, a brown beard going down his chin, touching the tip of his shirt, made sure his hat was smooth on his head with one hand while swinging the wheel with the other, settling into a parking space. He took out a clipboard, setting it on the head of the wheel.

Without wasting any time, Conrad began walking to the driver in the truck, waving his hand in the air, trying to get the man's attention, which he eventually did, the man nodding his head to an old rock song.

Once he finally noticed Conrad, he turned the car off by twisting the keys, opening the front door, and sliding out.

"Conrad Brookes?" He waved the clipboard in the air, meaning for him to take it and sign the paper attached to it. Conrad quickly took the clipboard, signing his name with the blue pen stuck to it. The driver, who Conrad had several phone conversations with, snatched the paper, carefully looking over what Conrad had written as if he needed to find the slightest error. Conrad began tapping his foot out of impatience, but was relieved when the man finally gave a slow nod then gave him instructions about what time the vehicle had to be returned, how to steer the wheel properly, and to not get any scratches on the car.

Conrad was afraid there'd be a few more than tiny scratches on the car. He'd even say a completely damaged vehicle by the time he returned it. That is, if he ever got a chance to return it.

Chapter 21: Confronting the Crime Boss

Before Conrad could ask how they were going to reach the lair, his dad hauled Vanish off the ground, who groaned as if something caused him a lot of pain. It was then Conrad noticed the blood running down both of his hands, dripping to the ground. Cosmo had shot him in both of his hands, and Conrad could only imagine how much it would hurt to clap them together.

Once they all climbed in to their seats, Conrad climbing into the back of the truck next to Victoria and his mom, while Vanish was

dragged to the smaller vehicle with a gun pointed at his head by

Cosmo, they set off to the road which would lead them away from the

forest and back to the city.

The scenery consisting of maple trees and some oak trees caught

Conrad's attention, not remembering seeing any of the land the first

time they drove past it, his mind being in a million other places. All

he knew at the time was he had to get to the Disappearing Hole, and

fast. Nothing else mattered.

All of a sudden, Beverly's bright, cheerful smile popped into his

head, and the urge to get back to Buzzard instantly became his num-

ber one goal. It didn't matter he would vehemently curse the island

every time someone mentioned it. He just needed to get back, and

Conrad would never tell anybody why, either.

After what felt like a million hours later, Conrad's mind swimming

in a fog of trying to prepare himself for what was coming up, their car

finally slowed until coming to a complete stop, Magnum's building

looming in the distance, giving off the impression of business workplace.

One car sat in front of the building, and Conrad started wondering where everybody else was at. A tap on his shoulder made him realize his mom was trying to get his attention, taking his time to turn his head to look at her.

She ran a hand through her hair then began in a soft, almost coaxing voice, "That school you go to, anybody catch your interest, yet?" At this point, Victoria was staring at him, too, with a toothless smile on her face. Conrad began tapping one finger on his lap, muscles tightening, remembering when Ethan started to describe Alpine's muscle freezing Gift. If he didn't know what it felt like before, he certainly knew now.

"Uh, no," Conrad shook his head, uncomfortable. "Wasn't really looking for anyone. I got other things to think about."

A grin flew up Silence's face and she exchanged a knowing look with Victoria.

"Well," she said, running both hands through her hair this time. "I guess that answers *that* question."

"Listen, I said I wasn't-" Conrad begin to grouch, but didn't get to finish. The left, back door to the other car began to open, and Vanish made his way out, Cosmo right behind him, still pointing the gun at his head. The front door to the lair opened, a woman in a navy blue business suit exiting, clutching a binder under her right arm. She immediately came to an abrupt stop when she saw Vanish and Cosmo, her mouth, covered in beige lip gloss, hanging open.

Conrad put his fingers on the button which rolled the window down, making sure there was a small crack between it and the sill. He leaned closer to the door, listening.

"Vanish, what's going on?" The woman threw one hand up so she was clutching her curly hair, bottom lip dropping down and dark blue eyes opened wide.

"Just get back inside, Celia." Vanish flicked his fingers forward and backward. "Don't come back out here."

"No, you stay where you are," commanded Deputy, stepping out of the car. "And why don't you use the pretty little earpiece you got on to let your boss know we've arrived." The woman named Celia held a hand by her ear, lips moving as she let Magnum know what was happening. Before she could say anything else, a shot rang out from

Cosmo's gun, which he had pointed upward towards the roof.

Celia screamed, jumping once in the air, hands in front of her ears.

If Conrad didn't know any better, he'd say someone had been walking on the roof of the building, wielding their own weapon. Key word: *Had*. He didn't know if they could even stand up now.

Another shot rang out in the air, and Conrad couldn't help but grin. Knowing the crime boss's henchmen were being taken out, one by one, erased any of the nerves he felt before they arrived. First, he'd hidden behind a tree at the sound of the gunfire blasting into the forest. But now, he kept his vision straight ahead, where all the action was taking place.

Swinging open, the front door to the lair burst forward on its hinges, slamming into the wall. And who should come rushing out but the crime boss, himself, hands raised above his head.

"Whoa, whoa, whoa!" shouted Magnum, appearing scared and angry at the same time. "What's going on, out here? What do you want?!"

"Nothing, really," said Deputy casually. "Just wanted to show you what happens when you threaten my son." Magnum shook his head, then let out a slight laugh, arms still held above his head.

"Come on. Deputy." Magnum had a nervous grin going up his face, hands opening as if he were being held at gun point by the police. "I would never threaten this guy." He pointed in Conrad's direction. "I've known him for too long. He's like a nephew to me. A part of the family. My little partner in crime-"

"Okay, now you're just getting on my nerves." Deputy whipped a pistol out of his pocket, aiming it at the crime boss.

"Woah! Hey!" shouted Magnum, taking a step forward, to Conrad's surprise. "We can come up with some kind of a deal. You know, since you guys are back, you may need my help with keeping the vigilante's eyes off of you. Staying hidden. And I got the perfect devices for that. All you have to do is put the gun down, relax, come inside, and we'll get you all set up." Magnum shrugged, sliding a foot across the ground.

Deputy remained still, appearing to think it over. Finally, he motioned for Cosmo to step forward then turned his attention to the car Conrad was sitting in, eyes squinting. Victoria went out first, then Silence afterward, Conrad just now noticing she held her well known flame thrower. Magnum eyed the weapon in her hand, moving his teeth from side to side.

"Alright." Deputy nodded. "As long as my gunman and Silence can
go in first."

"Sure, sure," said Magnum, taking a few steps back so he was by the
door. *Criminals*, Conrad thought in irritation, thinking someone's life
had to be on the line for them to get anything done.

"And tell Celia here to let everyone know to release their weapons.
That'd be mighty kind of you." Magnum motioned for Celia to come
forward, impatience dancing in his eyes. She flung open the door,
probably scared and just wanting to go home. Conrad wouldn't be
surprised if that was the last time the crime boss ever saw her again.

Once she was done telling the workers to put down their weapons,
Celia stood next to the entrance, keeping the door open by standing in
front of it. Deputy began motioning for them all to enter, only stopping when he met Conrad's gaze. He stared at his son for a few more
seconds, lips pursed, before he finally made a decision.

Deputy swung his hand forward and backward, meaning for him to
hurry up. Conrad pushed the car door open, jumping out onto the
gravel. If anything, it was a relief to be out of the stuffy car, out

where he could breathe some fresh air.

He didn't let nerves get the best of him, even though it felt like he was going to vomit out what little bits of food he had left in him. Well, okay, maybe he was being a bit over dramatic, but that didn't mean he felt ready walking into the lair.

The old building stank of mold and dust, old paper sitting on the abandoned desks taking up the majority of the room. Vanish had once told him the building used to be a clothing factory which closed down due to the company receiving low wages, and instead of relocating, the manager simply decided to close everything down.

So, Magnum eventually took over the space and claimed it as his own, recruiting whoever he could find to work for him. Conrad often wondered what would happen if an undercover cop came by, saying he needed a job.

Magnum would merely bark out a snide laugh before claiming he had eyes in the back of his head. He'd catch that guy in a second. Just watch.

Chapter 22: Visiting a Vigilante

As they made themselves comfortable at one of the desks, Deputy
stood next to Magnum as he pulled down a screen showing a map of
Cove City, circling different areas with a long stick he picked up off
the floor.

A strange scene suddenly caught Conrad's eye. Cosmo and another
man who held up a pistol, where giving each other the evil eye. A
grin sometimes spread up Cosmo's face as if he was just messing
with him. An amused smile went up Conrad's own face, enjoying

what would have been a showdown if Deputy and Magnum weren't there. Before he could continue to witness what he thought to be a show of some kind, Magnum let out a piercing whistle, clapping his hands together once before saying, "You three, over here!" He pointed to a few of his workers in the back of the room, gesturing to them by waving his hand forward and backward.

Silence held the flame thrower up higher on her knee, having had taken a seat at the same table as Cosmo, who still had his eyes on the man who held his gun like he was afraid of it slipping out of his hands.

"Everybody, get up," instructed Deputy. "And let's go. We need to stock up, and get moving." Conrad stood up from his seat, relieved to finally be leaving the lair and venturing outside. Although, if he really thought about it, going outside made him more uncomfortable. Even though they had more room to run, the bosses accomplices could be hiding anywhere, and he knew he wouldn't be able to see if someone came out of nowhere to attack.

He chose to climb into the car he had rented, Silence following behind him while Johnny went inside the other vehicle, no doubt holding on tightly to the steering wheel.

As soon as they went back on the street, another car, a black Ford, inched up next to the car his Uncle Jonny rode in, and Conrad felt his stomach drop. As quick as a flash of lightning, Cosmo leaned out of the back seat of his side of the car, pistol aimed at the mysterious visitor who cinched next to them.

'Bang, 'bang' 'BANG.' Cosmo showed no mercy as he let the bullets fly. The unknown car to the left of them sped forward, the wheels screeching on the gravel. Conrad held his breath as they nearly ran into a car in front of them, managing to keep a steady pace instead of swerving out of control. Silence, his mother, put an arm around him as her eyes began narrowing. Conrad had to resist shaking her arm off, not appreciating being treated like a little kid. As soon as Silence's eyes widened again, the unknown car burst into flames, and began to swerve left and right before finally crashing into an oak tree.

He swerved into another lane on his right, not surprised when another vehicle came on their left.

"Figures," grouched Conrad, jerking the wheel so they were speeding down the middle of the road. Of, course they'd leave the car

Johnny was in alone and rush at him, instead. They knew who the faster driver was, and it wasn't him.

He put his foot on the gas pedal more firmly as another vehicle sped up behind him, getting closer by the minute. *Okay*. He looked to the side of himself, saw an opening then forcefully turned the wheel so they were in the lane to the far right.

"Conrad, what are you doing?!" his mom screamed, but he simply tuned her out, not looking to be distracted by anyone or anything. He just had to keep up with his uncle.

It didn't take long for the wailing of a police siren to sound off behind him, and the car behind him slowed its speed until they were simply going slowly down the road. But the first car speeding beside him kept up its pace, eventually making its way closer and closer.

Twisting the wheel so they were no longer next to the dangerous vehicle, Conrad again pressed firmly on the gas pedal, making their car zip down the freeway, passing other people in cars who must have thought he was crazy.

He was pretty sure an old lady in a beat-up sedan gawked at him when he sped by, eyes bulging out of her head. Just as the vehicle which refused to let him get away came closer again, a puff of smoke rose from the front of it.

The smoke soon turned into bright red flames reaching the car's front window. The driver began twisting the wheel in what seemed to be a panic, the police car catching up to him as he began to slow down. *Thanks, mom.*

Grinning, he also began to slow down as soon as Johnny did, keeping up with him but not going at high speeds like before. The whirring of blades on a helicopter reached his ears, and he couldn't help but guess they were a news crew reporting on the crazy driver behind him. Now far behind him.

He couldn't help but wonder if freeing his parents from the Disappearing Hole already spread out amongst other criminals, criminals who didn't appreciate the fact their worst enemies were set free. So, the race to capture Deputy and Silence had officially begun, along with their two accomplices who used to be from the Caplin Gang.

Spotting the green sign which read Cove City Exit, Conrad swung the wheel so they ended up in the far right lane along with Johnny, putting his foot on the brake as they came near a red light.

The skyscrapers in the city shone up ahead, the sun's rays bouncing off their surfaces, reminding Conrad of a sparkling light show in the city when they celebrated a holiday, fireworks popping in the sky.

They ventured down the street which took them directly to the city, pedestrians scurrying along the side-walks, swinging shopping bags by their legs or talking on cell phones. Following his uncle into the back of an alley which had a parking structure for a local restaurant, Conrad came to a stop next to a brick wall, avoiding knocking into a trash bin along the way. Unbuckling his seatbelt, he quickly opened the car door, jumping onto the gravel. He hears doors slamming shut behind him as everyone else exits, keeping his eyes forward as Johnny and Cosmo came out of the vehicle in front of him. Stepping out of the car, Deputy opened his fingers wide then began pushing his arm forward, meaning for Conrad to stay where he was at. Conrad nearly let out a frustrated groan, a little tired of being treated like a measly toddler.

All three of the men, along with Silence, disappeared around the corner, leaving him alone with Victoria, who continued to sit in the back seat. He had to wait for what seemed like a million years before

Silence peered from around the brick wall, motioning for him to join them. And he promptly did so, hearing a car door shut behind him, guessing Victoria finally got out, too.

Once he came around the corner, Deputy had what Conrad could only guess to be a map of the city, pointing to different areas.

"Johnny, Cosmo, I want you guys to go to the downtown area of Cove, where one of the vigilantes is keeping watch. Silence and I will be there with you shortly. Just need to pick up a few things. And as for our vigilante friend…well, you know what to do with him. Go make his day."

Both of his uncles nodded before hopping into the car, Conrad and Victoria following after them, Conrad's nerves performing flip flops and backflips again. Go make his day. He knew that couldn't mean anything good.

Chapter 23: Making Rigel's Day

More skyscrapers poking up into the atmosphere flew by the car in a blur, the downtown of Cove City finally surrounding them. Pulling his legs up on the seat and wrapping an arm around them, Conrad began inhaling and exhaling out his nose, trying to calm himself down.

Their car, slowing its speed, came to a stop next to a convenience store, a man holding a stack of papers in his hands standing still in front of the shop. Leaning so he could stick his head out of the window, Johnny began waving at the man with the papers.

"Ey!" called Johnny. "Do you know where we can meet one of the vigilantes patrolling the area? We're tourists, and, uh, would like to see one of them." The other man, who looked like a regular civilian to Conrad in his blue jeans and tie-dye tee, started pointing to the top of Flagship. "You can visit him up there. Rigel, I think his name is. You might have to wait. There are other people there, too. Hoping to take a picture with him." Nodding, Johnny began pulling away from the sidewalk so Flagship could be closer, parking near the entrance.

Dusting himself off, Conrad also hopped out of the car along with everyone else and started walking to Flagship, feeling relief when they simply strolled through the front door instead of having to bash it open because it was locked.

Not looking around at the scenery inside the building, Conrad didn't slow his pace except when they made it to the elevator, quickly walking inside and pressing button number thirteen. The very top floor.

His stomach hosted a show of butterflies as soon as the elevator started its ascent, watching the number by the door flash cherry red whenever they came up to a new floor. 'Ding!' Conrad kept his eyes on the door as it began to slide open, disappearing into the slot it came out of.

He stumbled forward, Cosmo having had pushed him in the back, forcing him to leave the elevator. A warm breeze immediately hit him in the face, the weather bordering on a hot summer's day. Conrad had to remember they were back in Cove City where it never seemed to cool down.

He could see Rigel right away. His red and black suit complete with a mask which had a beak extending out of it like it belonged to a vicious bird of prey. He kept statue still, staring at the city below.

Johnny took his time walking up to him, hands in his pockets, exuding nonchalance.

"No pictures, right now." Rigel crossed his arms, eyes narrowing. Conrad thought he probably just wanted to go home. "I have a job to do and don't need anyone bothering me."

"We just wanted to see one of the famed heroes." Johnny shrugged, not uncrossing his arms.

"I'll give you five seconds to get away from me," Rigel snarled, letting his arms dangle by his sides. "Five…"

"Or what?" Johnny laughed, widening his arms. "You gonna show us your super strength that you got from the school up north?"

"I think I will." Rigel stepped forward, hands in the shape of claws. "And you better show Warren's school more respect. The kids up there are taught every lesson they need to become great vigilantes-" Without wasting any time, Victoria moved closer to Rigel, hands on her hips, a scowl on her face.

"So, I guess the kids at the other school don't matter, huh? Or did you forget about them?" Rigel's forehead crinkled, eyes narrowing once again, confused by Victoria's abrupt question. "What other school? You mean Warren's Refuge of Neglected Gifted?" He let out a snicker, clasping his hands together. "We had to find out how to get the negative attention off some of us Gifted in *some* kind of way. Point the finger at someone else. And it's working pretty well if you ask me. Especially since we got pyroglees and canids hating each other."

Gritting his teeth, Conrad couldn't help but think about all the ways he could burn the man into dust, leaving no trace of him except a black line where he used to be standing. He couldn't help but think Warren didn't care who was on his team of vigilantes, even if they had a big mouth, and were pompous and arrogant like Rigel. As long as they could take down criminals and earn the city's respect then they had nothing to worry about.

Shaking his head, Johnny had his upper lip raised before spitting out, "You're freakin' crazy."

Rigel let out another laugh before saying, "Maybe I am, but at least I have a good future ahead of me. Can't say the same for those dirty, rotten, kids at the Forgotten Gifted-"

Conrad knew he was going to say more, but before he had the chance, Victoria reeled back her arm, fingers stretched out to as far as they could go. Hand now wide open, she didn't hesitate to push her hand out so Rigel was shoved by her Gift and flew backwards off the building, plummeting to the ground. Even as he fell, Conrad could hear his cries of terror.

Chapter 24: A Sob Story

A 'bang!' came from way down below, Conrad peeking over the
edge to see what had happened. A car alarm rang at the same time he
glanced back at the angry woman, staring at her in shock.

"You know…Victoria," said Johnny with an uneasy smile on his
face. "We could have done it." He pointed at himself and Cosmo. "I
mean, we got the weapons and stuff. You didn't have to-"

"I know," said Victoria, flipping her hair over her shoulder. "He was
just getting on my nerves."

A scream raced through the air, panicking voices coming afterward, no doubt talking about the man who came flying off the top of the building. The now dead man.

All it took was for Cosmo to say, "Uh, we better go," for them to hurry back inside the elevator, push the button going to the first floor, and scurry out into the building.

A man behind them let out a loud shout of, "Hey!," but that wasn't going to stop them. Making a mad dash outside, an all-black Porsche slid in front of them, and Johnny's excited cry of "Oh, yeah!" took up most of the small area they came into.

Deputy and Johnny instantly switched places, Conrad and Silence taking the back seats again, Cosmo sliding next to them. Conrad looked around for Victoria, watching her hop into the truck he had rented for the time being. They were all ready to go.

In true Johnny fashion, he began to forcefully twist the wheel around, getting to the right spot, before jamming his foot on the gas pedal. Their car now flying backwards, Conrad flinging back in his seat, Johnny now had them going forward, heading out of the down-town area, speeding past all the shops.

The wailing of sirens following behind them didn't make any noise this time, filling Conrad with some relief they had officially avoided any detection.

"Johnny, stop a little ways up here." Deputy began pointing up the street in the middle-class area of Cove City. "I need to pick up one more thing." Pulling up to a couple of little shops, Johnny finally put his foot on the break, coming to a stop next to a sidewalk.

Deputy got out with little fuss, hardly making a sound as he started walking to one of the stores. Rolling down his window, Conrad strained his ears as what sounded like a woman newscaster on a tv above one of the stores began explaining the events of the day, including Rigel's fall to his death.

"Heartbreaking news tonight as we go over the fall of one of Cove City's bravest and much-loved vigilantes, Rigel." Shots of police cars and ambulances hurrying to the scene of the crime, along with clips of crying pedestrians. One woman holding a tissue up to her eyes, tears streaming down her face, explaining to the camera how much Rigel meant to her and her family.

"It's just..." She wiped at her nose at the same time Conrad stepped out onto the sidewalk, glaring at the television. "…hard to hear, you know? My kids are going to be devastated. They were big fans of him."

Hmm, thought Conrad in disgust. *"Well, that's just too bad."* The news woman held the mike under her mouth, cherry red lips dipping as if she was fighting off tears.

"This is truly heartbreaking news," she said as if it were the most gut-wrenching story she ever had to report about. Conrad had a feeling Rigel was really popular amongst the chicks in his city, and nearly gagged. "The police are still researching the area, trying to figure out what could have possibly happened. As you can see, patrol cars are still circling the streets, trying to figure anything out."

Suddenly, a man with an apron tied around his neck didn't waste any time stepping next to her, fumbling with his fingers. "I was in my shop when some people burst through the door. I swear to you, they looked just like Deputy, Silence, and the rest of the rest of their gang." Conrad spit on the ground, disgusted. His dad hadn't even been with them when they rushed into the shop. He probably saw Silence and just assumed Deputy was with her. The newscaster woman suddenly turned around as if startled, the microphone she was holding snatched from her, someone holding it up to themselves. Bertram Swift was now holding the mike, glaring at the camera.

"Whoever did this," he snarled, eyes narrowed. "Will not be spared from our anger. We will catch them, and show them what happens when you mess with us."

"I'm telling you," the shop owner came back into the shot, waving his arms. "It was Deputy and Silence. Who else could it have possibly been-?"

Forcing his hand onto the man's neck, Bertram's fingers pinched, making the shop owner choke, he began saying again, "We got rid of those two years ago, so, naturally, it would make no sense for them to appear again, would it?" He waited for the now scared man to nod before releasing him from his tight grip.

Tuning back to the camera, Bertram began dusting off his suit, saying, "As I said, we got rid of those two, already. There is nothing to be afraid of. And Rigel, I promise you." He lowered his head. "You will be avenged." Conrad had to admit, watching Bertram take off into the sky just by stomping his foot on the ground was kind of cool.

Setting him on fire in a storm of flames would be awesome as well.

Raising his arm in the air, hand balling into a fist, Conrad couldn't

help the small amount of laughter escaping from his throat.

Wafting into Conrad's nostrils, the strong smell of smoke took him

back, but the surprise which overcame him soon turned into relief, en-

joying the bitter smell. Deputy had come out of one of the shops, a

cigarette between his lips, holding a new pack of cigarettes.

"What have I told you about smoking in front of my son, Carson!?"

Silence stuck her head out the window, eyes on the brink of turning

blood red. Conrad knew she had to be steaming mad to call him by

his first name instead of the pin name he always used. "You put that

out, right now." Instead of listening to her, Deputy took another drag

before blowing the smoke back out, not appearing to care in the

slightest how mad he was making his wife.

An amused grin on his face, ruffling Conrad's hair, he started push-

ing him towards the car and bent his head down so he could get back

into his seat.

Stepping back into the passenger side, slamming the door behind

him, Conrad heard him ordering Johnny to take off, his uncle taking no time in doing so. The wheels screeching against the road, the car zooming onto the street again. Conrad's hand gripping the arm rest, he began wondering where they could be going to this time, multiple images floating threw his mind at once.

If anything, they might be heading to another bank to rob, sending another wave of butterflies into Conrad's stomach. It would be just like his dad to force him into something like that.

His hand gripping the arm rest even harder, he then remembered they're plan of getting rid of all the vigilantes, too, thinking about who could be next on his dad's list. Well, he guessed whichever vigilante came to the bank they were going to would never see the light of day again. He let out a puff of air, nerves running haywire in his stomach, a man's voice coming from the radio.

"Breaking news, it has just been reported well-known vigilante, Rigel, has fallen to his death from his position on top of the Flagship Building a few hours ago. We don't know how, yet, but suspicions are coming in about Deputy and Silence look-a-likes. Uh, Yeah, Look-a-likes." Conrad could only imagine Bertram standing next to him, mouthing what to say, giving him a mean look in the process.

"We'll be back with more details, so be sure to stay on this network."
'Click.' Someone had turned the radio off. He didn't know why. The reporting of the fall of Rigel was filling him with too much amusement.

The ride to Westchester bank took more than ten minutes, Conrad noticing a lack of cars in the parking spaces.

The building stood at only on one floor, its windows shut and surrounded by metal barriers. Its double doors flapped shut whenever someone walked through them, and Conrad noticed people mostly came out.

People had already figured out about Deputy and Silence being released, not wanting to be anywhere near a place which could be a target.

Johnny and Cosmo came out from the car, Johnny sliding his feet on the ground as if wiping dirt off of them. He began unwrapping an object covered in white paper, tossing it up and down in his hand when he finished. He thrust back his arm, swirling his wrist around and around before throwing the object, chucking it so it flew towards the bank. Oh, man.

It blew out an explosion as soon as it hit the ground, which Conrad knew made the glass in the windows rattle, without a doubt drawing everyone's attention, the car shaking from side to side from the force of the blast.

The front door to the bank slid open with a 'bang!', a man wearing a security guard's outfit running out afterwards. Grinning, Johnny waited for the man's attention to fall on him, and once their eyes fell on each other, the poor security guard fell to the ground, knocked unconscious.

One right after the other, more security guards came out of the building, rifles held high, scowls on their faces. Conrad watched them all make eye contact with Johnny, one by one, falling to the ground afterward once they did, guns slipping out of their hands.

"Hmm," said Silence, scooting over to the door and slipping out, smoothing her outfit as she went. Conrad figured it was about time he got out, too, unclicking his own seatbelt.

Silence looked over at him, paused with her hand on the doorknob, then beckoned for him to join her. Conrad let out a sigh, knowing it was now or never.

Chapter 25: The Robbing of Westchester Bank

Getting his feet to move was more difficult than he thought it would

be, feeling as if his shoes were glued to the ground. *What's the matter*

with you? Don't you want to experience this? Immediately changing

his pace to a much quicker walk, Conrad finally made it to the bank,

watching as his mom twisted the doorknob before going in, Conrad

after her.

Inside the bank, clerks who were working behind mahogany desks

wore light grey shirts and hats, either quickly typing on computers or helping customers. Snapping at one of the female employees, a man with a phone in his hand was trying to move past the lady grouching at him. Getting back to his house didn't seem like a likely possibility. Especially with the angry woman in a rouge dress barking at him about receiving her money. Conrad would have felt sorry for the younger man, who was clearly panicking, as if he had bigger things to worry about.

Conrad went backwards until his back made contact with a wall, putting his fingers against the cold structure.

Johnny was in the far right of the room, hands behind his back, Conrad knowing he was keeping the baseball bat out of sight. On the opposite end of the room, Cosmo also kept his weapon from out of site, focusing on what appeared to be nothing.

Silence kept her slow walk as she went by him. Deputy, he just now noticed, stood near the front of the bank, next to the registers, in everyone's sight, in Conrad's opinion.

What was going to happen next absolutely floored him, but it wasn't until Jonny walked to the middle of the room, facing the cashiers, did he prepare himself for what was about to go down. Like loud rock music had gone off, drums being the main musical instrument in the piece, the heads of the cashiers fell onto the counters with a 'Thump'! Conrad couldn't hold back the grin climbing up his face.

"Alright, everyone!" Deputy went to the middle of the room, resting his foot down on a chair in front of a computer. A couple of women let out screams, while a few more people dropped low to the ground, hands covering their heads. "We just need for you to stay down, be patient, while we clean this place out. Shouldn't be too much, right? No, course, not."

Swinging his baseball bat, Johnny walked over to the passed-out workers on the counter, peering down at them as if to make sure nobody was still awake. Cosmo had his gun pointing at anyone who moved, shoving the end of it into people's heads if they wouldn't hold still.

Deputy spoke a second time, leaning hands on the leg he had bent on the chair. "Now, we don't want to take up y'alls time, so we'll try to make this quick."

A man with a fading hairline and a checkered patterned top moved across the ground, fingers gripping the smooth floor as if it would take him on a ride out of the bank, and back home. Conrad could im-

agine his wife with a black and white apron, cooking him his favorite

meal. But before he could get any closer to the door, Johnny's base-

ball bat came slamming on the ground, right in front of his face, the

'clonk!' noise it made seeming to echo around the room. Yep, Home-

run Johnny. Irritate him, and get smacked in the face with the bat.

Conrad grimaced, not wanting to see such a brutal beat down.

This time, instead of calling his name, Deputy simply pointed at

Cosmo then to a closed door behind him. Turning around, Cosmo be-

gan walking to where he thought he was supposed to go, Conrad as-

suming all the bank vaults were somewhere behind the room.

His father's gaze fell on Conrad, eyes narrowing and leaning his

head on his shoulder, deep in thought. Finally, he motioned for Con-

rad to go with his uncle, not looking away from him until he actually

picked up his feet and left his spot.

Once again, Conrad's shoes seemed to stick to the floor, every step

as if his feet were stuck in quick sand. He watched Cosmo barge in-

side, Conrad guessing he had probably picked the lock in no time at

all. Arms beginning to shake from nerves zipping through his body, he eventually found it in himself to open the door.

Office desks and chairs were on both sides of the room, leaving a clear path down the middle, where Cosmo fiddled with something on the wall across from where they came in. A door blending in with the wall itself. With one final wrench on what Conrad guessed to be the doorknob, Cosmo was finally able to enter the secret room.

Keeping up with him, Conrad peeked inside the room, and almost stomped his foot in disbelief. Steel bank vaults on both sides of the walls, with giant locks hanging off of them. Wasting no time, Cosmo went to every lock, sticking what Conrad assumed to be a thin device in the bottom of them then twisting it so they clicked open.

Cosmo's attention fell on Conrad, waving the boy over and saying, "Come on, come on, come on. We got no time to loose." He tossed an empty bag at him, wider than Conrad's chest, longer than him length wise. Conrad opened his hands, catching the loads of cash Cosmo threw at him, dumping them in the bag like he found a pile of gold.

He didn't want to admit it, but the job itself was feeling pretty enjoyable to Conrad, who was loving the smell of the money wafting out of the bag. Bringing the bag up to his face, sniffing the interior, he really began to see what the big deal was.

  Stopping what he was doing, Cosmo stared at Conrad for a quick second, an amused smile on his face. The smile turned into a frown as he said, "Let's go, let's go. Quickly." Clutching the top of the bag, Conrad ran to the way out along with his uncle. The scene in the bank was pretty much how they had left it. People laying on the floor with their hands over their heads, a woman in high-heeled shoes sniffling on her hand, sometimes bursting into sobs as if she didn't think she'd live to see the next day.

Chapter 26: Frightening Ophelia

Deputy put his hand in the air again, waving it from side to side then
pointing to the front door. Their mad scramble out the building took
less than a few seconds, Johnny pulling up in the Porsche Conrad's
dad had stolen.

Johnny took off before Deputy could even tell him to go, yanking
back the stick shift, stomping on the reverse pedal, spinning the car
around so they were going straight forward. Conrad gripped the edge
of his seat when he started to slide forward. He wasn't going to slide

off. Nope. He'd stay in his seat. Even if he had to clutch the edge with his fingernails.

Once Johnny spun them around, getting them out of the parking lot, he slammed his foot on the gas pedal, making the car skyrocket back onto the street. Conrad sucked in more air as the car's wheels screeched on the road, unsure of where they were going. All he knew was, he better hang on, and he'd better hang on tight.

"Where to, now, Boss?" Johnny inquired, not taking his eyes off the road. Conrad knew his dad had responded, but the shrieking of police sirens muted most of his hearing. Flicking his head back, arm up against the top portion of the seat, Conrad could see blue and red lights flashing behind them. They had been spotted. Probably by the cops who were called by someone who worked at the bank. He didn't know when it happened, but now they were on the run for their lives.

Suddenly, like a breath of fresh air, the sirens behind them faded, throwing the boy's head into a whirl of confusion. Why had they given up the chase? And where was Victoria at in all this? He couldn't see the truck anywhere.

"We got company." Conrad could see his father drumming his

fingers on the window sill. "White van. Right behind us." Once again, he tried to look over his seat, but saw nothing but the dark window behind them. His dad must've had eyes in the back of his head which could see just about anything.

"Pull over, right now," demanded a woman calling from a speaker, Conrad recognizing the voice as one of the vigilantes. Well, if she thought she could keep up with them, she was in for one heck of a ride.

"Driver, pull over immediately. This is your final warning." Johnny let at a laugh as he continued to speed down the road, only slowing his pace when they came upon what appeared to be two mountains up ahead, a thin line, which Conrad knew to be the road, snaking between them.

Instead of decreasing his speed, Johnny sped to the line between the mountains, twisting the wheel so they went off road, to the mountain on the left. They came to a stop when a pile of boulders came into their line of site.

After throwing off his seatbelt, Deputy jumped out of the car, arms wide open, a smile showing the teeth in his mouth. Conrad put a clasped hand to his forehead, thinking his dad was waiting eagerly to get shot. Geeze, why didn't he just run to the van and beg to be arrested? It would make since.

The front door to the van burst open, a silver boot stepping out onto the dirt.

Just as Conrad suspected, Ophelia was the one to step out of the car, clad in a neon blue, spandex jumpsuit, taking baby steps towards them, fear shooting from her eyes, the corners of her lips dipping low, reminding him of a toddler getting ready to start crying. He couldn't believe she was the only one they sent, in a rickety old van, the blueish green lines of paint fading from the sides.

"You're back…" She ran a hand through her bleach blond hair, coming to a complete stop.

"Missy, of course, I'm back!" barked Deputy. "What would this city be without me?"

Out of the blue, Ophelia's head was yanked back, Silence having had snuck behind her and grabbing a fistful of her hair, yanking it down.

"Hello, Hun." She had no qualms in yanking Ophelia's head back a second time, causing the woman to let out a shriek, hands clasped together in outright terror. "Since you seemed so desperate to catch us, how 'bout we put on a little show for you?" Flicking her head to the side, her eyes fell on Ophelia's vehicle. *Oh, yeah. Here it comes.* Rubbing his hands together, regarding what was sure to happen in anticipation, Conrad began counting down the seconds until the car's destruction.

"One," he murmured, but that was all it took. Just one second for the car to burst into flames, causing Emerald to release another scream, swatting at the air, coughing as the smoke came too close to her mouth.

Taking several steps forward so he could be in her face, Deputy had no problem leaning closer to her, their faces inches apart. A squeal came out of Ophelia's mouth, twisting her head away so she didn't have to look at Deputy. Putting his hand on her cheek, he forced her to look at him, not minding the tears running down her face, the cries coming out of her mouth.

"Now, you listen to me, darlin'." He stroked her cheek, making

Ophelia shake in her stance. "You go on and give your leader a little message. You tell him it really is us, and nothing can stop us from ripping this place into shreds."

Chapter 27: Visiting the Boss of the Caplin Gang

Grabbing her by her shirt, Deputy pulled her to him before shoving her away, Ophelia stumbling backwards before taking off, taking out a cell phone, holding it to her ear. Conrad could hear her shouting into the phone even as she got further away.

Bertram… He wanted to spit on the ground again but at this point, nothing squishy was in his mouth except for his tongue. The guy didn't even bother riding with Ophelia in the car chase, just sending her out, by herself, into the clutches of some of the most feared criminals in Cove City. And for what? So, he could sit back and relax in his high chair and not have to deal with anything? Or was he really so afraid of them, staying back and lying to the press about how there was nothing to be afraid of was all he could do?

They got back inside the smaller car, Deputy shuffling them along, urging Conrad not to waste any time.

"To the Caplin Gang, then?" came Johnny's voice from the front.

"To the Caplin Gang," agreed Deputy, nodding his head. Staring out the window, Conrad wondered what they possibly wanted from his uncle's old gang. Where they even in California? And if so, why had they relocated? He decided to ask Silence the same question whirling around in his mind.

"They came over here to avoid the cops," she promptly answered him, nodding. "And to keep running their illegal businesses. I think we're going to see them to try and negotiate more deals."

"You mean, they'll actually listen?" Conrad let out a snicker, throwing his hands on top of his head. "After two people who used to work for them, betrayed them then disappeared? This is just-" He would have said crazy, but now that he thought about it, 'crazy' sounded like too soft of a word.

Psychotic? No, something more intense. Going completely out of their minds, lunatic crazy? Yeah, something like that.

"We're not going to go barging in there, son." A snicker came out of Deputy's throat. "Just making a quick stop, collecting some things, and we'll be out." Conrad ran a hand down his face, thinking they'd visit every criminal in Cove city before they actually made it to Buzzard Island again. Before *he* made it back to the island. And the only way to do that was to go back to Magnum's lair and grab Vanish.

He had no idea how he was going to explain to Beverly what he'd been up to the whole time he'd been away. Or even to his brothers, for that matter. He already knew a bunch of annoying questions would be thrown his way.

They slid through the downtown area once more, the same shops open, some selling jewelry hanging on strings, others touting the best food anyone could get their hands on. Conrad could have done without the food, especially since the aroma of pork sizzling on a skillet sent his stomach into a growling dance.

"You hungry?" Silence cast him a look filled with worry.

All he felt like doing in that particular moment was flick his eyes at her, not in the mood for any long conversations, even if the only word he had to say was 'Yes'.

"We'll stop and get you something to eat in a little bit. Just hold on." Smoothing the ends of her hair, she finally sat back in her seat, fingers still clutching the ends of the right side of her dyed hair. Dying it black had always been something she'd been interested in, preferring the smoky color over her natural maple brown locks.

A couple of weeks after they jumped into the Disappearing Hole, Conrad had done nothing but sit in his room, mourning, wishing he'd been allowed to jump into the stupid hole, too. After he finally got up from his bed, he slow-walked to the bathroom in the living room at Liz's house.

He'd opened several drawers before he found what he'd been looking for. He grabbed the two new packs of black hair dye and poured it all over his hair, not caring in the slightest if some slid down his face.

After Silence vanished, Liz was allowed to keep anything which had belonged to her daughter. Conrad didn't know what it would be like if they saw each other again, or if they'd even be happy. All he was certain of, was his grandmother was in for the shock of her life.

They went into a parking structure for a wine shop, squeezing in between a Ford and a Mustang.

Once again, Conrad was ordered to get out and go inside with them.

Bill's Winery had an old western build, walls appearing to be worn thin, fake cobwebs hanging off the structure, and a poster of a cowboy lifting his boot in the air as if he were going to tap his foot, was hanging from the window.

Conrad never would have guessed the place was run by a gang running a fake business, but then again, he never would have even glanced at the place twice.

Stepping inside, Conrad's eyes fell on the cases of wine bottles pinned against the walls, smelling dust and the ancient wooden furniture drifting around the room.

'Tap,' 'Tap', Tap.' Computer keys, in use by a woman with a net hanging over her short hair, a light brown tunic tied around her neck.

"Hello." She blew a strand of hair out of her face, eyes still on the computer screen. "How may I help you-" As soon as she set her sight on who came in, her jaw dropped, eyes widening in shock, or fear.

Conrad guessed both, Deputy moving to the front so he was standing

across from her.

"Hi, Darlin'." He snatched a bag of sour candy off the counter, rip-

ping it open. "Is your boss in right now? I'd like to speak to him."

"He-he won't be in 'til a little later. W-why don't you come back in

two hours and I'll-"

"Ah, little girl." Deputy moved his hand around inside the bag, pick-

ing two pieces and popping them into his mouth. "We know he's back

there hiding in his office. I'll give you four seconds to go on back,

and bring him out.

Spinning on her feet, the cashier lady took off running to the office

behind the register, her legs almost getting tangled together. Conrad

had to hold back a snicker, now anticipating the boss's arrival.

Walking out of the office, round spectacles on his eyes, irritation

wrinkling his face, the boss steadily made his way forward, some-

times casting glares at the room he came out of. When he turned to

look at them, the glare transformed into a draw dropping, eyes gaping

open in astonishment, hand grasping his chest, surprise. Mouth shak-

ing as if he wanted to say something, he finally brought himself to bring the words out.

"You two." He pointed two fingers at Johnny and Cosmo, sliding his shoes to the left side of the room as if he were planning to bolt to the front door. "What are you doing back here? Get out of my shop. Take your country friends and go."

"Come on, boss." Johnny raised both of his hands, shrugging.

"No, no." He was pointing at the front door, now. "You don't work for me, anymore. I'm done with you. I told you this, before. Go."

Deputy walked in front of the frightened boss, who, by now, had sweat forming on his forehead. Taking two alarmed steps back, the boss, who's name tag read Eric, thrust his opened hands in the air.

"We just need two little things from you," explained Deputy. "After that, we're gone. Their names in your inventory, delete them. All traces of them, including their birthdays, must be deleted. Oh, yeah, it's going to be a long ride back home. So, we need some change." By change, Conrad already knew he meant a big sum of money. Rubbing his hands together, the amount of money dancing inside his head, an-other toothless smile spread up Conrad's face.

Thinking he was becoming another version of his dad didn't bother him at all. The manager opening the cash register only adding to his glee. His excitement ran out the door once an important memory came to mind. There was still much to do. And he couldn't see himself getting it done without two people.

Chapter 28: Calling on Vanish

The bumps on the road made him hop in his seat when they finally drove out of the parking lot. Conrad didn't know how he'd put his words together in the crisp morning air, or even where to begin, but he had to start somewhere.

"Hey," he said, able to string some letters together. "I need to go back to Magnum's place and uh…ask if I can use Vanish…for something." Deputy turned his head over his shoulder, forehead wrinkling, staring at his son in confusion. "I mean, if it's too much I'll just go back, myself."

"No, actually," began Deputy, scratching the bottom of his chin. "I was thinking of dropping you back off over there, anyway. Are you planning on going back to the island?" Conrad let out a relieved sigh, happy things were going a lot easier than he'd previously thought they would.

"Yeah, at least for a little while."

"Huh." Deputy glanced over at him, again, raising his eyebrows. "Looks like Vanish will have his work cut out for him. And when you get there, remember to keep a sharp eye out for the vigilantes' arrival. Note everything you hear them say then report back to me. Vanish will be there with you, and will tell everything to Magnum."

"Will he?"

Deputy instantly turned to look at him, raising his eyebrows. "He will if I tell him to." And with that, he twisted back around in his seat, once again leaving Conrad with an amused grin on his face.

...

The ride back to Magnum's lair seemed to last a day to Conrad, who eventually shut his eyes and fell asleep. Their car pulling into the driveway, going over a speedbump, rocked him out of his slumber, remembering where they were at, nerves creeping along his insides. He didn't know why visiting the crime boss all of a sudden made his heart race, because it never made him nervous before.

In fact, he used to look forward to it as a little kid. Now, seeing the building of the crime lord made his skin crawl, sent nausea bubbling in his stomach. *Just one more time. Get this crap over with, one more time.*

Johnny made sure to park on the side of the curb, not actually in the parking lot this time. Two men in all black suits and wearing shades came out of the building, eyeing the vehicle closely, speaking quietly to each other.

Instead of hearing the click of a gun being loaded, the door to the passenger seat opening and closing was all that he heard, watching as his dad began walking to the building with his hands half raised.

The two men wearing shades cautiously made their way towards him, one of them feeling along a pocket on his pants, alerting Conrad he might be getting ready to pull out a pistol. Pointing to the car, murmuring something in the man's ear, Deputy kept his attention on the guard in front of him, only looking back once to beckon for Conrad to step out of the car.

Jumping out, Conrad shut the door quickly behind him, wondering what he could possibly say to come off as convincing. This time, picking up his feet and moving his legs forward caused him no problems, casually walking to the guards like he was walking to his own house.

As soon as he reached them, Deputy spun around and headed to the front door of the lair, Conrad following behind him. Instead of knocking, his dad merely swung the door open, making it smack against the wall.

Entering the office space, he noticed less people sat working at the desks, typing away on keyboards. They must have come a little too early.

Right on time, exiting his own office, Magnum approached them with a frown on his face, arms moving back and forth in his hurried stride.

"Deputy, what-" began Magnum, but Conrad wasn't going to let him finish.

"I need Vanish's help to get back to buzzard. And to the city, afterwards." Scratching his head, Magnum stayed quiet for a few seconds, before belting out a laugh. "Sure thing, kid. Just wait for Vanish to make his way in, and we'll set everything up." Not knowing whether to be filled with relief or not, Conrad decided to take a deep breath and stay calm, clenching his fingers by his sides.

Not saying another word, Deputy's eyes fell on Conrad then swiveling himself around and heading back out the door.

Magnum had Conrad take a seat in a lone, white chair in the front of the room, where he could sit back and relax. But, the longer he waited for Vanish to walk through the door, the more uptight he was beginning to feel.

Once Vanish finally came strolling into the building, holding a briefcase and wearing a striped blue and silver tie going down his shirt, Conrad let the comforting warmth of relaxation embrace him.

It didn't take long for Vanish to stop in his tracks, eyes inspecting the room until he eventually spotted Conrad. Heaving a long sigh, shoulders lifting up and down, he started walking towards the boy. It was apparent he had already been briefed about his next assignment.

And he wasn't happy about it.

Chapter 29: Returning to Buzzard Island

"Buzzard?" He abruptly asked, a disgruntled agitation to his voice.

Nodding, Conrad kept his gaze on the man's eyes, not looking away.

"You couldn't catch a boat or somethin'?" Instead of answering, Con-

rad narrowed his eyes, tired of considering burning the hair off the

man's scalp if they waisted any more time. Shaking his head, Vanish

then held out his hand, wiggling his fingers.

Reaching his own hand out and placing it on top the man's upturned

hand, the rush of air blew past him at all sides, lifting him off his feet, a flash of colors zipping past him. Feet dropping to the ground, head still spinning, dropping to his knees, Conrad flipped his head up at the sound of a wave crashed onto the shore.

Turning his head to the side, water rolling onto the sand on the beach, only filling his insides with the same queasiness he experienced before the boat ride. If only they didn't land so close to the ocean.

"How long do you need me to stay here, for? Because I got other things to do." *You mean like going back to the lair and hanging out?* Keeping his mouth shut had never been more difficult, but managing to keep the words inside his head was something he could do.

"Now, let's go over the schedule." Hands planting on his hips, Vanish's eyes bore into him. Flicking sand off himself, rising to his feet, Conrad met the man's glare so they were staring at each other. "What time do you need me to bring you back and where do you need to go?"

"To downtown Cove City." If the man didn't wipe the dirty look off his face, Conrad could do it for him by throwing his fist at his nose. "And I need to grab two more people at the school. And listen to what

Bertram has to say when he gets there. It'll probably take all day."

"Well, hurry up then. Like I said, I got things to do."

"Yeah, yeah." Stomping on the sand, Conrad hands flying into his pockets, he made his way to the fence blocking the edge of the school. The cool breeze doing nothing but reminding him, yet again, he was on an island.

A fence guarding his entrance did nothing but make him throw his head back in annoyance. They would. They honestly would block his only way to the school by planting a stupid wiry structure in his way.

Grabbing onto the wires, hefting himself up, Conrad put all of his strength into pulling himself to the top, thinking his brothers better be happy to see him when he came inside. Taking less time going down, Conrad simply jumped to the ground when he got to the middle of the fence. Same as he usually did.

Silence was the only thing flowing across the school grounds, the occasional 'clink' clink' from the swings in the little kids playground providing musical clanging. Kneeling low to the ground, gripping part of the fence with one hand, Conrad stopped himself from jumping into the air with joy when the bell's shrieking pierced the school grounds. Lunch time.

Picking up his feet, he made his way to the top of the field, searching for the other two boys. Ethan made it to the field first, unzipping his backpack, digging through it, pulling out a binder with the school's name on it scrawled in the center of it.

Conrad stuck two fingers inside his mouth and gave their signature whistle, which consisted of one quick, "Phee, phee," and a long, "Pheeee." Spinning around in shock, Ethan's eyes widening, he caught site of Conrad in a second, raising his hands above his head as if to say, "What the-" Taking his time, bringing his feet slowly to the ground, Ethan hesitantly stopped in front of Conrad.

"Finally," Conrad exhaled, opening his mouth to say more but stopping himself when noticing Timothy still hadn't made it in front of him. Throwing his hands on the top of his head when noticing Timothy in a full-on lip-lock with Nova at the top of the field, he left the whistling to Ethan, who had to try three times before he got the other boy's attention.

Timothy spun away from Nova with a droopy grin on his face, stumbling across the grass as he tried to make his way to them.

"Was I interrupting something?" Conrad said as Timothy came in front of them.

"Nope." A nervous laugh escaping from his throat, Timothy smoothing his hair down. "It's all a part of the deal, Conra-Oh, hey, you're back."

"Man, both of y'all make me sick." Crossing his arms, Ethan's lips dipping into a frown, he continued ranting, "As soon as I go through a breakup, you just have to-"

"Remember, Ethan." Waving his hands in front of his face, Timothy then pointed at his brother. "This is all part of a deal."

"Can I get a word in!?" Conrad had enough, wringing his fingers together. "I have to get back on the beach with you guys or Vanish won't help me, Magnum is going to accuse me of lying to him, and part of my plan will be ruined!"

"Woah, woah, woah." Ethan put his hands outward, reminding Conrad of a cross guard. "Vanish is here? And what do you mean Magnum is going to be upset? Am I missing something? What the heck is going on?"

In as little time as he had, Conrad began to explain, as fast as he

204

could, everything he had been through, including releasing his parents from the Disappearing Hole.

"Why didn't you tell us about any of this before?" Ethan cocked his head to the side, tapping his foot. "We would have helped you a long time ago."

"Yes, and Locke isn't sure he should miss turning in this homework. He means, he's missed so many assignments already." Conrad never was one to beg. He actually was insulted by the word, finding it a mockery if somebody used it to describe him. But, oh, well. Begging, it was.

"*Please*." He put enunciation on every part of the word, even though he wanted to choke after doing so. Ethan, smoothing his blazer, came forward, and Conrad dreaded the stinging 'no' he knew was coming.

Chapter 30: Bertram's Infuriating Speech

"Okay." Ethan shrugged, fingering the straps of his backpack. Turning his head to look at Timothy, he began tapping his foot. Twisting his neck as his wide eyes fell on both Ethan and Conrad, Timothy's shoulders went down, heaving a sigh.

"Alright, Locke's coming. But just so you know, Magnum better have one of his hypnotists control the memories of our teachers at this school, because Locke is NOT failing all his classes."

"But, before we go, man." Scratching at the back of his head, the tone in Ethan's voice took on a somber quality. "Mr. Summer's told us Bertram and K.O.R.E. are coming here to talk to us. And I have a feeling it's not going to be one of those nice, sit-down chats."

"Back to the dorms then." Clapping his hands together once, turning around, Conrad began heading back to their room, glad he didn't have to say much to try and convince them.

Keeping low as they scrambled back to the dorms, Conrad began wishing for, of all things, to be short again, so it would be easier to hide himself. But as they made their way to the dorm rooms, he found ducking to be the new norm, shoulders hunching towards each other. Cursing under his breath and ignoring Ethan and Timothy smirking at his irritation, he ran to the steps as soon as he saw them, almost trip-ping on one in the process.

Once the sun started to go down, making its decent, a woman's bored sounding voice came through the speakers.

"Students, come down to the stage next to the cafeteria. Our im-portant visitors have made it here." Rolling his eyes, shoving the door to their room open, Conrad had to restrain himself from causing any more noise to break out, used to being forceful with things instead of gentle.

Leaving their rooms, chatting to one another in excitement, it was clear they already knew who their special guests were, Conrad half expecting to hear a marching band heartily welcoming the vigilante's appearance.

Yard duty teachers waved them forward, pointing to the rows each student should go through. Conrad took a seat in the third, Ethan and Timothy sitting next to him. He thanked God none of the teachers pulled him aside, recognizing him as the student who started tossing fire on the school grounds.

Mr. Summers, the school's principal, came up on the stage, clutching his navy blue tie in his hands, occasionally rubbing the fabric, making sure it hung straight down over his honey yellow top. Conrad remembered Ethan comparing him to some bird called The Yellow Rumped Warbler, and ever since then, every time he saw the man, he couldn't get the dang bird out of his head.

"Everyone, your attention is mandatory." Mr. Summers tapped on the mike, lips pursing. "As you know, we have a special guest, tonight. So, everyone please welcome the man who protects our city, every day. Put your hands together for Mr. Bertram Swift." There was more than putting their hands together. Cheers and whistles also bombarded the entire field, the excitement flooding Conrad's ears, making the urge to blow up the entire place a fervent want.

Stalking out to the mike set up for him, thin arms stuck to his sides, similar to Gary's own pouting stance, Bertram then snatched the mike out of its holder. A breath of air came out of his lips, sky blue eyes roaming over his entire audience.

"As you may have heard." He ran a hand down the front of his suit, eyes continuing to look from side to side at the school kids. "Rumors are going around about the release of Deputy and Silence from the Disappearing Hole out in the Redwood Forest. But I will have you all know, right now, this isn't true. We put them away years ago, in a place where they'll never return." Conrad didn't mind allowing a chortle to burst free, hitting a fist against his chest to control himself.

"And if we find out that one of you was responsible for this, there will be a steep price." A minute ago, he claimed the idea of them being loose to be pure folly, now it certainly had to be one of their

faults. How fast the truth about how he really felt came out.

Conrad ceased his laughter. "We know none of the kids at the

School for the Gifted would have done something like this, commit-

ting such a horrible crime."

The field had fallen silent, nobody saying a word. Looking around

once more, Conrad couldn't help but notice all the excited smiles had

disappeared, replaced by glares, kids nudging each other, pointing to

the man they must have finally realized was not on their side. Sud-

denly uncomfortable, Bertram cleared his throat.

"As I was saying, this was a horrible crime. One which we will find

the culprit of by any means necessary."

"And Rigel, too?" A kid sitting in the front row asked, raising his

hand. "Will you guys find who murdered him?"

"Oh, yes." The fury in Bertram's eyes rivaled any time Conrad saw

red, himself, quelling the urge to smash anything in his way. "As I

said before, the cause of his death will not go unanswered. We'll find

out about this, I can promise you that. Now, on to more important things." Smoothing his tie, huffing so his chest puffed out, he took a deep breath before opening his mouth.

"As of today, you'll continue to practice controlling your Gifts with the shield-There is a shield here, right?" He looked to one of the yard duty teachers who was standing next to him. She quickly nodded, nervously fiddling with her fingers. "Also, you'll start wearing the bracelets we swore to give you as adults."

The groans coming from all the students was palpable, another reminder of the dislike for the man in front of them.

"We gotta wear those dang things *and* deal with the shield?" Ethan snapped, throwing a hand up in the air. "What the *heck*, man?" Conrad couldn't look him in the face, feeling like the new restrictions was all his fault. Getting off the island became more than just a want, but a fervent need.

"Another thing." Clasping his hands together, Bertram's speech became ultra-serious. "Several guards will come onto the island regularly to see how you're doing. They are also allowed to use force if they feel it's necessary. Thank you." Whirling around, he stormed off the stage, not caring who got in his way.

Chapter 31: A Close Call

Getting up from his seat, with what might as well have been a
weight on his shoulders, Conrad followed the yard duty teachers waving their hands to the dorms. He would have kept going if the familiar
sound of someone's gasp didn't stop him in his tracks.

Mouth opening in shock, leaning on her heels and toes, Beverly's
hands flew up to her mouth, Conrad already knowing what was going
to happen even before she took off running. Throwing her arms out,
jumping in the air, Conrad caught Beverly. Taking her arms from

around his neck, comfortable with staring at him, her dark brown eyes peering deep into his.

Not wanting to waist any more time, Conrad's hand went behind her head, pulling her in for a much-needed kiss. Something inside him instantly went off, and the urgency to get back to the beach came barreling inside him, stampeding like a group of wild horses.

"Beverly." His hand came down from around her neck, carefully putting her on the ground. "I have to go."

"Wait, Conrad-" Beverly let him go, face a wall of confusion, mouth opening as if she meant to say more.

"I'll be back, I promise!" Pushing his legs to go into high gear, the fence in his sight, arms pumping up and down, Conrad had to ignore Beverly calling out his name a second time.

Leaping onto the fence, the climb upward did little to slow his pace, Sticking the tip of his shoes into every hole, grabbing onto the wires, getting poked by a loose wire in the process. His brothers scrambling up behind him was like a chorus of soothing music to Conrad, telling him he 'wasn't in this alone, anymore.

Hopping to the ground, the smell of ocean water and plant life flowing through his nostrils, Conrad was running like a track star in the Olympics, putting his shoes to the test. The stronger the dang smell of ocean water became, the faster he went, not even checking to see where Ethan and Timothy were during his mad scramble.

When the piles of sand came up on the West side of the island, he slowed his pace, taking deep breathes, clutching his sides. As he suspected, Vanish was nowhere in sight, probably having had clapped his hands and disappeared, arriving back at the lair.

Shoving his hand inside his pocket, fingers searching for the mini phone Magnum had given him. Finding the hard object, pulling it up by his ear, and pressing the button which would make the phone place the call, he listened to the ringing, waiting for someone to pick up.

"*Alright*, I'm on my way," Vanish snapped through the speaker, his voice giving Conrad a headache. Putting one foot on the sand already made his legs hurt, thinking all the exercises in the world wouldn't be enough to make running on sinking terrain comfortable. Heck, he'd even take running a mile around a track compared to dashing across the sand. And on top of everything else, he could hear waves crashing onto the shore.

Wanting to kick his shoes off and run back home flooded his mind, but it suddenly occurred to him how foolish the idea was. He was on a darn island. There was no way he could run home without drowning in the water.

"Man, where's this guy at?" He heard Ethan snap somewhere behind him. Just as he spoke, a loud 'Pop!' almost took over all of the sounds on the beach, startling a flock of birds who were walking near the water.

Glaring at them, taking few steps forward, Vanish's hands were held outward, preparing to clap them again. Motioning for Ethan and Timothy to hurry up and join him, Conrad ran to the man who would get them off the island, shaking his legs after coming to a stop, flicking drops of water off them.

It took exactly two seconds for Vanish to clap his hands together, flinging them up in the air, and a whirl of different colors zipping past Conrad's vision put his head into a sea of confusion.

...

A loud 'smack!' sounded once their shoes landed on the marble floor, the lights in the lair flickering to a dim level and back to its' bright-

ness.

Dusting himself off, Conrad managed to stand up straighter, the tap

of shoes on the floor floating into his ears. He looked behind himself

at Ethan and Timothy, who came to stand next to him.

"Alright, you guys, follow me." Beckoning for them to get a move

on, Vanish led them to the door at the end of the hall, turning the

knob with his left hand.

Making their way inside the room with a long table in the middle of

it, eight of Magnum's workers sitting around it along with the crime

boss, himself.

"Well, well." Standing up from his seat, throwing the paper down he

was showing his workers, a smile easing its way up his face, Magnum

then folded his arms together.

"What did Bertram have to say at that school of yours? Anything in-

teresting?"

"Just that we have to keep using the shield." Conrad tried not to

snarl his response, but he couldn't get rid of his anger. "And we have

to start wearing…" Shaking his head, he almost snapped his eyes closed, sure they were on the brink of turning blood red. "These de-vices which stop our Gifts from coming out." Nodding his head, a more serious expression coming over his face, Magnum said with a laugh, "Well, at least you don't have to worry about it anymore, do you?" A couple of the man's workers didn't stop their own laughs from bursting out their throats, cackling and slapping the table. "You're a free man now, ain't ya? What more do you have to worry about?"

Marching to the table, boots stomping on the clean floor, Conrad said in a low, breathless voice. "It's not me I'm worried about. This guy has the power to keep us from using our Gifts. All of us. And we can't do anything but listen to this maniac!" This time, Conrad was the one who smacked his hands on the table. No. More like slammed, causing some of the workers to jump out of their seats, startled.

"Settle down, settle down." Magnum moved his fingers up and down at the men who jumped up from their seats, meaning for them to sit down. "I know the situation is hard but we have to look on the bright side. As I was saying, you're basically a free man now. You can do whatever you want. I know other kids at your school will be affected, but just think about it, you're still home free."

Gritting his teeth, Conrad had a hard time believing the stupid man couldn't understand how the whole thing was infuriating. And not just to him but everybody else at Forgotten Gifted. The angry looks on their faces said it all.

"So, it doesn't matter about the rest of us." Stepping forward, shaking his hands as if trying to subdue his Gift, Ethan had no problem about slinging his backpack to the ground. It made a hard 'thunk!' when it hit the floor.

"Oh, you again." Magnum's eyes narrowing, he threw Ethan a dirty look. "Anyways, I was planning on offering some help to you guys, but it's hard to tell if you really want it or not…" His eyes drifting down to the backpack, he then snarled, "And don't be throwing your stuff on my floors. I'll kick you out."

Conrad had no choice but to start nodding, figuring it couldn't hurt staying on the man's good side, especially since they needed all the help they could get.

Focusing on Conrad, a grin traveling up his face, Magnum spoke, "I know this lady not too far from here. She's one of my hypnotists. Can make people see things differently, throwing their minds out of wack. It's up to you if you think she'll be useful."

Not bothering to open his mouth and speak, Conrad simply moved his head up and down, curious about Magnum's mysterious friend. "Her place is just up the street, about a block from here. Now…" Magnum paused, crossing his arms. "Did Bertram say anything else about protecting the streets? Like the places he's going to go looking for crime?"

Conrad saw the bottom of Timothy's mouth move from side to side, getting ready to say something. Conrad fervently shook his head at him, desperately warning him to keep his thoughts to himself. Unfortunately, the moron had other plans.

"Actually, he made no mention of any other ideas he wanted to carry out. Perhaps you should give him a call and find out for yourself." Hand slapping against his face, Conrad thought the idea of sliding to the floor in a ball of embarrassment was all he could do. That, and fear for the other boy's safety.

"*You.* Aren't you the one I said I never wanted to hear talk again? And you dare open your mouth?" Magnum nodded at one of his gunmen, meaning for him to come forward. Liking to think he was as quick as a bullet when he moved, Conrad leaped in front of Timothy, blocking him from anyone else's site. Ethan was quick to do the same so they created a wall in front of their brother.

"Remember, my dad isn't too far away," he spat with plenty of venom in his voice. He didn't know what it would take to get the man's attention off Timothy, but if he had to threaten him by mentioning Deputy then so be it.

"Well, look who I've gone and upset." Magnum let out a snicker. "Alright, kid. I'll leave your friends alone. Just remember, I've got my eyes on you." Two of his associates, the men in black who brought them in, rushed in front of them, shoving them towards the door.

Chapter 32: Denial

The cool air brushing against his face once they made it outside did absolutely nothing to cool his heated temperament. It actually made it worse. Like, a trillion times worse.

"Get off me!" Snatching his hands out of the guards reach and shoving the man to the ground, he had no remorse watching the man scooting away on his back, his eyes widening as his vision went to the boy's eyes. *Of course.*

"Hold on, just a second." Another one of Magnum's security came out, his black suit unmoving in the wind, almost like he had ironed

the whole thing flat. Lifting his sunglasses up, he said nonchalantly,

"The boss wanted to give you this. Said you might need it." Snatching

the paper at of his hands, which they hadn't even bothered to fold,

Conrad set his eyes on the black ink scribbled across it.

'The map to Sadie's Establishment,' was printed at the very top, the

print out of the map beneath it.

"Oh, yeah." The same security guard, who was really beginning to

get on Conrad's nerves. "The boss thought you might need this if

you're going back to Refuse. A little battle plan, if you get the gist."

Snatching the papers out of his hand, flipping them over, his eyes

scanning over the font and pictures on the paper.

How to break inside the vigilantes headquarters, what to do once he

got inside, and sketches of people, who looked like they had Gifts, us-

ing their powers to fight off attackers. Yep. Battle plans. Passing the

papers to Ethan and Timothy, Conrad watched as the truck he rented,

which was long past due, drove into the driveway, going into a park-

ing structure. Conrad instantly saw the head of the woman behind the

wheel, instantly thinking *Oh, no.* His vision went to Ethan, who blurted out, "Who is that?" *Oh, no. Oh, no. Oh, no. You just* had *to*

tell her about me. Conrad resisted bad mouthing his mom, clamping

his mouth shut.

Victoria hopped out, hand on the door for balance before swinging it

shut. Looking around, she finally noticed Conrad standing stationary

by the exit to the building, eyes directed at the pavement.

"Hey, little boy," she called, waving at him. Ugh, why did she have

to freakin' call him that? On top of everything else, he had to be re-

duced to a little kid again. "I heard you might need a ride. Just tell me

where you want to go."

If he glanced to the side of himself, he saw Ethan with a glare on his

face, a glare directed at him then at Victoria, his aunt. She stopped

dead in her tracks, hands flying to her lips when she spotted her

nephew.

Running with her arms wide open, Victoria pulled Ethan in for a

hug, sniffling and holding him tight. Ethan remained statue still, not

returning the warm affection in any way. Pulling away from him,

teary eyed, she put a hand to her mouth, observing her garden gnome

still nephew.

"I can't believe how tall both of y'all got. Oh, my goodness, gracious." A giggle came out, clapping her hands together in excitement.

"So, when you left and joined two bad guys, did you mean to put my parents in jail?" Ethan kept his voice low, not raising it to a shout like Conrad thought he might do. Staring at her nephew in shock, wiping the tears from her eyes, it took Victoria more than a few seconds to find the right words to say.

"Ethan, you know your mother and Ron mean the world to me. I would *never* do anything to hurt them…Or you. Especially you." Conrad didn't know what to do besides exchange a worried look with Timothy, both of them keeping their mouths shut.

"So…you really *did* know my aunt this whole time?" Ethan's eyes went back to Conrad, searching his face.

"Yeah, ever since I was little." He looked back at the ground, not knowing what else he should do to try and explain himself.

"Oh…" Ethan's eyes also looked downward at his sneakers which he moved from side to side. "You're my cousin, then? And not my brother?" Conrad let a slight guffaw escape from his throat before slapping hands with Ethan, patting him on the back afterwards.

"Do you want someone to drive you back to Refuse or you going to stay here for a bit?" Victoria waited for his answer patiently, a grin going up her face, looking to both Ethan and Conrad even though she only asked one of them the question. Conrad rolled his head around his shoulders, getting the tightness out of his neck, the sore area having had been there for a while. It was a huge relief when a 'crack!' went off in the area he wanted it to.

"Nah, I'm definitely heading back to Refuse. Got some things to finish over there with someone else." A remembrance of what else he thought he should say flashed in his mind, and he quickly blurted out, pointing at Timothy and Ethan, "Their coming, too. I think."

"Yeah, we're coming." Stepping forward, Ethan made sure his eyes staid straight forward, refusing to look at his aunt.

"Uh, we'll probably see you again, Victoria." Timothy saluted her, nudging Ethan in the arm.

"Uh…yeah." Ethan finally made eye contact with her, giving up on being a grouch. Conrad knew his brother couldn't stay mad for long, always finding it in himself to go back to his nice side. It completely flew over Conrad's head how he did it. When something or someone made *him* mad, he tended to stay mad.

Opening her arms, she started pulling Conrad and Ethan in for a hug, waving at Timothy to join them, not looking to exclude anyone. A swarm of relief flowed into Conrad when she finally released them, not just the hug getting on his nerves, but being squished up against Ethan and Timothy grating on his sanity.

As soon as Victoria was on her way back to her car, Conrad wasted no time in doing the same, digging the keys out and pressing the button to unlock the door. Twisting the key in the lock, he waited for the car to turn on before putting his foot on the gas, swerving out of the parking space.

"Whoa!" Timothy's panicked shout almost broke the windows, in Conrad's opinion, who didn't slow down until they were on the road again.

"You know, Locke is not a driver himself, but he can tell when someone's driving like a crazy person on alcohol! Geeze, when does this wild ride end? It's a wonder we haven't been pulled over, yet."

"Shut up!" Conrad gripped the steering wheel tighter, tempted to increase the speed, but he knew concentrating on getting back to the freeway should be his only goal.

"And who is this other person?" Timothy kept talking despite hanging on to the back of the front seat in fear, his left knee raised.

"Maddox." Conrad gritted his teeth, regretting saying the other boy's name, knowing he was in for an hour of questioning. The piercing of sirens on a squad car never rang out behind them, nor someone shouting on a loud speaker commanding him to pull over.

The lime green sign signaling the freeway entrance shown right in front of him, changing lanes until he drove into the one leading to where he needed to be. Now all he had to do was keep going until he saw the sign for Refuse.

"Man, I didn't even know you and Maddox were planning all this." Ethan shook his head, perplexed. "When did you guys even become friends-?"

"We're *not friends*." Conrad had to stop himself from twisting the wheel out of frustration, the day suddenly beyond a pain in the neck.

"Whatever, man." Ethan stared at the road in disbelief, right hand on the side of his forehead, drumming his fingers.

The exit sign to Refuse made its appearance on the right side of the road, signaling to Conrad he needed to make a quick turn, sometimes cutting other cars off by accident. 'Screeech.' The wheels wailed in protest, begging him to slow down. But he had to keep going, to make it to his town, or, as Magnum once called it, his future home away from home.

Chapter 33: Road Rage

Pulling into the town, an eerie air seemed to flow in and out of the vehicle, in through his nostrils every time he inhaled, and hovering around him once he exhaled.

Nobody was walking the streets, no cars driving by. Nothing. Conrad could only hear a few birds chirping, but that was about it.

"What's going on?" Ethan asked, voice coming out as a high murmur.

As soon as he said something, an older man came from behind a tree, where Conrad assumed he had been trying to hide. He picked up his pace when he laid eyes on the vehicle, pushing his legs to go into a dash, not merely kicking both feet up in an unstable run.

"Hey!" He called, nearly getting his feet tangled in his long, jean pants. It was no doubt to Conrad he recently bought them at a cheap, thrift store. "Are you Conrad? We were expecting you. Don't know what to do after K.O.R.E. came down to visit. Saying things like, 'We need to keep ourselves under control, watch what we're doing, or their going to shut this place down for good. What do they mean by that?" The man's forehead wrinkled, creasing his eyebrows.

Conrad had no doubt about what they meant, a searing hot anger kickstarting the surge of his Gift through his veins. Refuse would be closed down for good, so they could build something else in its place. What would happen to the townspeople, he had no clue. Which was why his arriving at the time when he did couldn't have been more of a relief.

"Get everybody back out here," Conrad instructed. "I want to show them a few things." Swiveling around on his heels, the man with the sweater raced off to the front of the town square, stopping in front of a bell, a dong hanging out of it. Three rough swings at the bell, pushing it with his hands, created the sound he wanted, the ringing sounding more like, 'Bong!' 'Bong!'

Townspeople carefully made their way out onto the street, keeping close to each other, some of them with their shoulders bumping into the person next to them. Aaron and Lauren also cautiously made their way forward, sticking close to each other.

"K.O.R.E and Bertram told us to not cause any disturbances." Lauren had her hands clasped together; shoulders hunched. "To not do anything which might cause suspicion. But I have a feeling you're going to tell us to ignore them."

"I'm going to ask you to do more than that." Conrad whipped out the paper Magnum gave him, the one showing ways to fight back. He handed her the paper, swiveling around after he did so. He could have sworn he saw her smile before he started to leave.

Bertram must have really scared them if they didn't say anything about Ethan and Timothy coming into their town unexpectantly, without permission.

The 'Scrunch,' 'Scrunch' 'Scrunch' of shoes walking on the dirt was the evidence he needed of Timothy and Ethan keeping up with him.

"Where to now?" Ethan was now right beside him, Timothy a little further back. "We came to the pyroglee town and everything. Do you need something else?"

"The stone," said Conrad, not bothering to look at the other boy. "It can suck the Gift right out of you if you say the right words."

"Ah," said Timothy, coming up beside them. "Similar to the Disappearing Hole. And where can we find said stone, sir, Conrad?"

"Closer than the Redwood Forest, out in no man's land. Another forest called Trials Forest."

"Something tells me this place isn't for people who get scared easily." Conrad didn't bother answering Ethan, guessing the boy already knew the answer to his own question.

"Huh, a place where Conrad can finally feel at home. Wonderful!" Timothy pumped his fist in the air, giving a little leap.

"Don't make me sock you." Conrad had to use all the strength he had not to drive his fist into the other boy's face. But if Timothy wanted a repeat of getting a bloody nose after being hit then Conrad would be more than happy to provide it to him.

Taking his keys out of his pocket, Conrad unlocked the car, swung the door open, and flopped into his seat. The car doors closing next to the back seats meant Ethan and Timothy had entered as well.

Twisting the key in the lock and pressing his foot down on the gas, Conrad had to do his best to ignore Timothy's shouts of protest as he sped onto the road, turning on the radio, making sure the volume blasted out the songs. He ignored the freeway to his right, choosing to go onto the highway, instead. A lot safer, or so he thought.

Right when his car turned onto the highway, another vehicle, swerving next to him, stuck close by his side.

"You know, them?" Ethan pointed his thumb at the car to the side of them, eyelids wrinkling.

"No," said Conrad, pressing his foot more firmly on the gas, making sure they left the other car behind.

"Aaaahhhh!" Timothy cried out, probably wishing he was back on the island where he'd be safe inside his dorm room.

As he thought would happen, the other vehicle increased their own speed, catching up to Conrad. *Here we go again*, he thought in aggravation. Except, this time, his mother wasn't with them to turn the other car into a pile of ash. Somebody didn't want him going to the

forest, and Conrad dreaded what else they might do to try and stop

him.

A window rolling down to the side of him, distracted him for a mi-

nute. He glanced to the side of himself, seeing Ethan stick his hands

out of the car. And like it had messed up wheels, the second car

swerved left and right, the driver losing control of the car before driv-

ing off the road, leaving a big pile of dust to rise up behind it.

"Geeze, man." Ethan's mouth flew open, gaping at the other car.

"Once again, Conrad, I have to ask, what the heck are you involved

in?"

"You'll find out." Conrad subdued a laugh, focusing on the road in

front of him.

An old, dirty sign with cobwebs all around it, told them the forest

was just five miles ahead. All they had to do was keep driving

straight. The scraggly trees, branches hanging down like long arms,

having gaping holes in the front like open mouths yelling at them to

go back. But he couldn't. Not if he wanted to accomplish what he was

supposed to.

And just like a crick in his neck he couldn't get rid of, no matter how many times he rolled his head around his shoulders, no matter what he freakin' did, another car started to follow after him, taking their time at first, as if observing his every move then speeding up so they didn't lose track of him.

"Shoot!" The shout came out of him as soon as he slammed his free hand on the dashboard, nearly missing the car horn. Ethan looked over at him in surprise the swung his head over his shoulder, trying to see what had made the other boy so upset.

"*What?*" Ethan rolled down his window again, peeking out of it.

"We're being followed again!" Conrad twisted the wheel so the car made a U-turn. That should make it easier to tell if they were, indeed, being followed. And just like he assumed, the silver Lexus spun around as soon as he did, picking up speed, not letting them out of his sight. Conrad slowed the car down until coming to a stop at the side of the road, this time basically giving the jerks who were following him a chance to do their worst. He was ready for them.

Chapter 34: Pesky Park Ranger

Slowing down would buy him enough time, that is, if Ethan was up

for what he had planned only a few seconds ago. Conrad pressed

lightly on the brake, easing to what appeared to be a stop.

One person driving their car honked their horn at him several times,

along with a few other vehicles trying to get by. All it was to him was

a useless noise he could care less about.

"You got this?" Conrad didn't even glance at Ethan when he spoke to him, simply drumming his finger on the wheel. Ethan kept quiet, rubbing his hands together, taking deep breathes.

"Oh, brother" said Timothy, lowering himself further onto his seat. To Conrad's annoyance, the sound of a seatbelt clicking into place reached his ears. How many times did he have to tell him? Well, at least Timothy had prepared himself this time.

Copying his Uncle Johnny, Conrad spun the car around so he was driving side by side to the other car, inches away from it. And to his relief, he didn't come in contact with anyone driving right towards him.

The driver was hidden behind a tinted window, which was alright with Conrad. He didn't want to see the driver's panicking facial expression when Ethan unleashed his Gift on him. Rolling down Ethan's window while the other boy took deep breathes, Conrad let his voice go as he barked out, "Now!" That was all Ethan needed.

Sticking his hands out the window, sitting up higher in his seat, he aimed at the other vehicle's wheels, twisting them so they were stuck in one position, making the car spin around and around in circles. Pressing his foot on the gas harder so he could zoom past the spiraling car, looking over his shoulder for a quick second, he saw the pursuing car spin off the side of the road before coming to a complete stop.

"Whoo!" Ethan raised both arms in the air, pumping his fist once before remembering he should take it easy after having used up most of his strength.

Timothy sat up straighter in his seat after being flung to the side when Conrad spun the car back around so they were going the right9 way again.

"Are we there, yet?" Timothy asked nonchalantly, tapping his foot. Conrad shook his head as Ethan let out a snort, leaning back against his seat and closing his eyes, most likely falling asleep.

Five more blocks down the road showed the entrance to the forest, some of the tree bark missing leaves, like they had no water to dig their roots into. The whole thing remined Conrad of a pile of tooth picks somebody had stuck into the ground and glued more sticks to the side of them.

He rapidly parked into a space where dirt covered the cement, red lines stretching to and fro, meaning he'd indeed drove into the parking lot.

After jumping out, Conrad stuck a hand into his pocket, moving it around until he found what he'd been looking for. The map to the cave his dad had given him. Ethan and Timothy came to stand beside him, looking over his shoulder at the paper. The scraggly, black lines representing the trails went different directions, some to the North, others turning Eastward, where a lake was supposed to be.

Conrad squinted his eyes at the map, searching for the cave. Suddenly, he felt someone poke him on the shoulder. Timothy then tapped the portion of the page which displayed what looked like a large black rock with an opening in the front. Conrad nodded then folded the map into fourths before stuffing it back into his pocket.

"East it is," said Ethan, scratching his arm.

"Right," grouched Conrad, ready to throw the map on the ground and stomp on it with his boot. The crystal *would* be exactly where the water was at. Why would it be anywhere else?

They started off walking through the many trees with hardly any leaves on them, and Conrad began to understand why the forest was seen in such a bad light. Not only were the trees bare, but a slow moving fog crept along through the air, while the other half drifted across the ground.

They traveled about half a mile before the sound of flowing water drifted into his ear drums. Conrad wanted to freeze, to stay in his spot and not walk any further. But once again, he silently told himself he needed to keep going. This was the only chance he was going to get.

Someone grabbed the back of his shirt, stopping him. Conrad looked back at Ethan in annoyance, wanting to keep moving forward.

Ethan slowly put a finger up to his closed mouth then pointed forward. Three men in baggy clothes, and wide brimmed hats, were unloading a few flashlights out of a truck along with some folded-up tents. The last one held out a big piece of paper in front of his face, which Conrad assumed to be a map of their own.

The three men didn't look up from what they were doing, two of them standing right next to each other, sometimes pointing at the cave. Conrad thought their attention would never go to them, until the man holding the map looked up, scanning the area, his eyes finally falling on them.

He called to his fellow workers, and when they glanced at him, he pointed at Conrad, Ethan, and Timothy.

Chapter 35: Competing for the Stone

A man in the same clothes as the others, an apple red shirt with sus-
penders hanging down it with climbing pants, started walking towards

them, hands on the belt holding his pants up.

Stopping near enough to them but also keeping a comfortable dis-

tance, his jiggly stomach hanging over his belt, his light brown eyes

went over all of them, the left part of his mouth rising in disgust.

"No kids allowed over here," he said in a grouchy voice,

straightening the hat on his head. "go back to your parents. I'm sure

they're looking for you." Like always, Conrad's, and he was sure

Timothy's eyes glanced at Ethan, watching him sigh before saying,

"Nah, man. They dropped us off over here. Said we could look

around for our school project."

"Oh, really?" The man crossed his arms, reminding Conrad of a dis-

appointed school teacher. "And what type of school project would

that be? No, wait a minute, I know. Finding some kind of rock in the

cave over there? Well, I'll be the first one to tell you the cave is

closed for the day. Off limits while we do some work inside it."

"You're not even a real park ranger," Conrad blurted out, a glare on

his face, not believing he had to deal with more nonsense. "Where's

your badge?"

"Right here." The man took out what Conrad assumed to be a fake

I.D. before shoving it into his pocket. If he refused to let them pass,

Conrad was sure he could push the overweight man out of his way,

and maybe step on his hand in the process. Yeah, he was getting *that*

irritated. Ethan averted his attention from the so-called park ranger to

Conrad, staring at his reddening eyes. He abruptly turned back to the park ranger.

"Come on, man, just let us through." Ethan widened his arms, hands open. "We won't be in there for that long. Let us do a little exploring." One of the other park rangers whistled, two of his fingers in his mouth, waving at the other worker to come and join them.

The man in front of them moved his head up and down at the other workers calling him before saying quickly to the three boys, "I gotta go make some rounds with the gentlemen back there. Remember, no going inside the cave. It's closed for the day." And with that, he whirled around, running back to his co-workers.

They watched as the three men walked further on the field, their backs facing them, the man who approached them occasionally turning his head around to see if Conrad, Timothy, and Ethan were still in the same spot.

As soon as the three park rangers walked so far away, they became invisible to Conrad, he took off in a mad sprint to the cave, not slowing down for Ethan and Timothy, just pounding his shoes on the grass, not looking back.

The dark cave, almost black, was curved on the outside, Solid rocks poking out of the surface of it. Their sharp edges warned anyone what would happen if they came too close. Probably a vicious stab in the stomach, if they were dumb enough to try and climb it. The wide opening extended like a large creature's open mouth, hoping to gobble anything coming too close. *The only things missing are the teeth*, thought Conrad, standing at the entrance, noticing the wet dirt at his feet was more firm, making it less complicated to step on.

Taking his time walking into the gloomy cave, Conrad kept his eyes roaming the interior for anything that might jump out at him, its claws raised and fangs bared.

Inside was exactly as gloomy as the outside, with very little light touching the rocks, a ramp going through the cavern, with rails tourist could grab onto on either side of them.

An idea popped into Conrad's head, and he instantly held his hand out, wriggling his fingers. A bright flame burst from his fingers, causing a spray of light to hit the cavern walls, lighting up the dark space they were in, and, his entire face.

"At least we can finally see where we're going," remarked Ethan, keeping by his brother's side along with Timothy.

Reaching into his pocket, Conrad dug out the map without touching it with his other hand, making sure not to reduce it to a pile of burning rubble.

"Hey." He held out the paper to Ethan. "Hold this, and tell us which way to go." Ethan took the map, unfolding it then staring at the picture.

"This say's we go up Common Lands, up these steps then squeeze through the rocks in the center." He nodded, already seeing the sign reading Common Lands in front of him, balanced on a stone peg, a red border surrounding the letters on it. Above it, hanging from a long piece of rope, as a silver pendant lamp, shining light on everything around it, making Conrad's Gift useless. He shook the hand which had flames shooting out of it, putting out the fire.

"Why would they need the lights on if they're not down here anymore?" Ethan paused, only moving his eyes to look around.

Yeah, thought Conrad, also observing their surroundings.

"Perhaps they're simply waiting for the cleaners to come in-" Conrad quickly put a hand over Timothy's mouth, sure he heard shoes tiptoeing on the cavern floors.

"This way," he whispered, going further into the cavern, not bothering to silence the sound of his shoes stomping against the ground. His hand on the cave wall, arm stretched out, the cold, wet surface on his fingers unsettling him, Conrad convinced himself to continue moving forward. *Go! Go!* The stone steps going up to Common Lands greeted him up ahead, a sight for sore eyes in the damp interior of the place Conrad wished he could disappear out of.

Climbing the steps took no time at all, Conrad keeping his hand on the black rail next to him, trying not to slip and fall. If he did lose his balance, he could at least count on his brothers to catch him. They better catch him. Sweat slid down his temples from the climb, breath coming out in huffs, swatting away the temptation of flopping down onto a step and catching his breath.

Once again, the 'Tap,' 'Tap' of Ethan and Timothy's shoes entered his ears, saying in a coaxing voice he wasn't alone. The last step sang to him in a heavenly voice, and he hopped over it, twisting his head from side to side. *The rocks in the center...There!* Legs moving before he even had time to think about it, arms flopping by his side, Conrad finally came to the rock walls spaced a few feet apart, slipping through with no problem at all.

Waiting like a trophy on a pedestal, encased in glass, was the ruby red rock he was looking for. Reaching the case, Conrad looked around at the glass, at the writing they had put next to it explaining the history of the stone, the powers it was supposed to have, like how it could reduce someone's Gift into nothing.

"You need this?" asked Ethan in disbelief, pointing at the stone, eyebrows raised. Conrad didn't say anything, feeling the casing, tugging it to see if there were any weaknesses.

"It looks like they set a guard around it," remarked Timothy, fingering his chin. "I don't know if there's any way-"

'Smash!' Conrad brought his fist on top of the glass, breaking it into little shards. An abrupt pain struct him in the hand he slammed into the case, shaking it in a desperate attempt to make his hand feel normal again. Ignoring the blood running down his fingers, to his palm and nearly to his wrist, Conrad wriggled the stone in it's place, before tugging it with all his strength. The stone ripped from its hold with a rough yank, laying in Conrad's hand, fingers clutching it.

"Huh,' said Ethan, eyes on the stone. "Guess we're in a lot of trouble."

"Nah." Timothy swiped his hand in the air. "Locke took out all the energy in the camera's once we came in here." Conrad stuffed the stone in his bag, zipping it back up and hefting it around his shoulders. Okay, so Liz wouldn't be seeing his face on the tv screen after he told her he wouldn't get in any trouble. Sweet.

"Thanks." The word came out more like a mumble, prompting Timothy to respond, "What? What was that?" He placed a hand beside his ear.

Conrad glared at the other boy, pretty sure Timothy was just dragging it on to be annoying. Or, maybe he really did have to speak up. Swallowing a mouthful of air first, Conrad finally managed to spit out afterwards, "Thanks!" not knowing how many times he could lose his patience in one freakin' day.

The good thing was, he didn't have to find out, the bad thing was, if it wasn't going to be Timothy who was annoying him, it had to be someone else. And that someone happened to be the park ranger charging into the cave, two other park rangers coming in after him.

"I told you not to come in here," he snarled, sunglasses hanging over his eyes, giving him the appearance of a googly eyed bug in the dark cave. "Get out, right now. Out!" His eyes then went to the broken glass case on the pedestal, mouth opening into a gape. The gape soon changed into an anger as he put his hands on his waist, puffing his chest out like he was getting ready to make a mad dash at them.

The tips of Conrad's fingers went from a cool temperature to just about burning the skin off his hands. Oh, he was going to make it out with the stone. Whether the park ranger liked it or not.

Rubbing his hands together gave him the strength he needed, filling him up with the warmth he craved. Clapping his hands together once brought out a spark of orangish red flames, so hot, he felt the heat on his cheeks.

Mouth dropping open in shock, the man started backing away until he was almost at the entrance to the cave, holding up a walky-talky next to his ear.

Flinging up his hand, Ethan sent the device flying into the air, eventually knocking into one of the cavern walls. Mouth now shaking in shock, bottom lip quivering, the man whirled around, kicking his feet as he sprinted out of the cave, crying for help.

249

All they had to do was glance at each other once before making their own escape. Conrad thought they took two steps in total outside, before a 'Bang!' went off. He had no choice but to throw his hands in the air.

Chapter 36: The Mysterious Vehicle

A man wearing camo pants and a white t-shirt held a pistol up so it was square with his chest, a straight haired woman standing next to him with one hand on her hip.

"Alright, son." He hocked a wad of spit onto the grass. "We know you have the stone, so give it here to me and there won't be any problems." Really? *Really*? Now he had to deal with this idiot on top of everything else?

"You can take the stone…after you pry it from my cold, dead, fingers!" The urge to stomp both of his feet engulphed him, telling him it was okay to have a temper tantrum like a little kid, 'cause he certainly deserved it.

"Fine with me." The man held the pistol so he had it pointing directly at Conrad. Ethan rushed to his brother's side, leaning next to him so he could mumble in his ear.

"Just give it to him, man. We'll take it back, later."

"I need this stupid stone-!" Conrad kicked a rock out of his way, considering throwing it at the man who randomly appeared out of nowhere.

"Yeah, but he's the one who has the gun." Conrad understood what Ethan was getting at. As soon as one of them raised their hand to use their Gift, the man would fire his gun, and he probably wouldn't miss.

Feeling around in his pocket, Conrad didn't pull it up again until he had the stone which could take people's Gifts away in his hand. He then stuck his arm out, the man eagerly opening his own hand so Conrad could drop his prized possession into it.

Raising his arm in the air, shouting, "Whoo!" he then spun around, running to the parking lot, his girlfriend keeping up with him in her flats.

"Does anybody know the number to You've Just Been Robbed? 'Cause, Locke is certain we've been, what do you guys like to call it? Oh, yeah. Jacked." Timothy wiggled his fingers, a spark shooting out of his pointer finger.

"Yeah, but we can catch up to them, right?" Ethan turned his head so he was looking towards the parking lot.

Instead of responding, as usual, Conrad sprinted towards the parking lot, pumping his arms up and down, breath coming out as huffs. He flung the keys out of his pocket, jamming his finger into the button which unlocked the door.

"Come on, come on!" He waved his hand back and forth at Ethan and Timothy as they opened the doors and scrambled into the car. Conrad almost didn't bother looking behind himself. But he had to. Spinning the wheel to the left, Conrad pressed his foot on the gas pedal, watching as the other car sped onto the road.

"Not today," He murmured to himself, speeding onto the road. "*Not today.*"

"Woah, Conrad!" Timothy yelled from the back seat. "There's a speed limit! Locke's going to throw up back here if you don't slow down!"

"Hmm," was the only response Timothy was going to get from Conrad once he sped up behind the other driver, eyes narrowed, mouth pursed into a thin line. If he wanted to play race car then that was fine. Conrad could keep up. He sped to the left when a Honda Civic drove straight at him, putting him in the lane he was supposed to be in.

"Ahhrg!" Ethan flew to the side on his left, bumping into the section which separated him and Conrad. He didn't know how long this was going to last, but a red light up ahead, stopping the Buick, gave him some relief.

He stopped right behind the Buick, both hands on the wheel, clutching the hard surface. Beside him, laughter bursting out in their car, Conrad turning his head to the side, looking at Ethan as the laughs continued to roll out of him.

"This is great, man." Ethan tapped a hand on his chest, gulping down air, reeling himself in from the onslaught of laughs which had taken over him. "But don't run into anything."

"Conrad, ignore the manic ramblings coming from beside you," urged Timothy, leaning forward so his head was poking between the front seats. "All we need for you to do is slow down." Conrad made sure to stomp on the gas pedal as soon as he saw the light turning green, tossing Timothy all the way back into his seat.

A gas station's blinking sign, welcoming anyone to fill up their tank, came up on the right side of the road, and Conrad, assuming, the Buick would stop there for a quick refill, kept his eyes on the car in front of him. Exactly as he thought, the car turning into the gas station was a blinking sign of relief, making sure he did the same.

Another car, an old sedan, chipping yellow paint drooping off all around it, pulling up into the gas station, and stopping beside a pump, as if the person behind the wheel wanted to rest instead of actually get out.

Eye lids squinting at the strange car coming from around the corner, Conrad didn't take his eyes off them, wondering what was going to happen as soon as the thief who took his stone let go of the pump.

Chapter 37: Future Vigilante and Future Outlaw

Nothing, at first. Tapping his finger on the seat, watching the man letting go of the pump, he started thinking about how he was going to fill up his own tank. He could always- Jumping out of the other car, a man wearing a black beanie over his head, grabbing the thief by both of his arms, he then put a wide-open hand to his head, shoving him to the ground, his legs appearing to turn into jelly.

Another beanie wearing numbskull also jumped out, rummaging

around inside the thief's car until he found what he was looking for.

Yep, the stone. It made Conrad wonder how many people were after

the rock, or why they even needed it in the first place. The man in the

beanie hopping inside his car, stating the engine, putting his foot on

the gas pedal then speeding away.

An idea hit Conrad in the side of the head once he saw the man who

stole from them rush inside to one of the stores by the gas station,

probably to report how he was maliciously robbed. Well, two times

was about to be a charm for him. Motioning for Ethan and Timothy to

join him, he sprinted towards the empty car in at the gas station, really

picking up his legs the closer he got.

Without thinking about it, Conrad jumped into the front seat of the

car, twisting the key, putting the vehicle in reverse, and slamming his

foot on the gas.

"Hey!" shouted an angry voice from behind them, calling out,

"Hey!" again when Conrad didn't stop. He didn't have time to feel

bad about robbing the man of his car, especially since he felt like he

was returning the favor.

"Oh, no!" shouted Timothy, who, to Conrad's extreme annoyance, was seated right next to him. "Time for another wild ride with Conrad."

"Really, Ethan?!" He barked, quickly looking over his shoulder at the culprit.

"Hey, he got here before me," Ethan protested. "What was I supposed to do when he got in the front?" *I don't know. Send him flying out of the car with your Gift?*

"Did you guys see where this guy went?" Conrad jerked the wheel to the side, remembering them driving straight down the road, but nowhere else afterwards.

"Locke saw them turn left up here." Timothy pointed straight forward, where Conrad had seen them drive off to. *So, you actually can be useful.*

Conrad considered turning the radio on, curious if they actually made the news or not. He twisted the dial until the news station he usually listened to came on, listening to the reporter talk about what the weather was going to be like. Dry and warm. Conrad pumped one fist in the air, finally hearing something that was to his liking. Dry weather. Yep, he could deal with that. He raced down the road, only slowing down when he drove a few feet behind the other car, thoughts

whirling, thinking everything he had planned was ruined because

some idiot took his stone. Some jerk who he didn't even know the ap-

pearance of.

He swerved the car into the right lane so he was beside the other

guy, who had taken off his beanie. Conrad could make out his squint-

ing eyes, cypress wood brown hair, moving his thin lips to speak to

his partner in the back seat, wearing an all black tee.

"Conrad, how many people want this thing, man?" asked Ethan,

eyes on the road.

"A lot, but mostly criminals who don't want the law's eyes on them.

Or the vigilantes."

"Is that why *you* want it?"

Conrad tightened his lips, unwilling to answer the question…until

his mind completely changed.

"Yes." And there it was, the answer where he admitted to his broth-

ers how he intended to stay in the crime world. Maybe it hadn't been

the best thing to say, since Ethan did plan on being a vigilante, him-

self, in the future. *Shoot.*

"You plan to become a criminal, too? Geeze, man. What can I do when I catch you breaking into a bank or something? No, what do *you* expect me to do?"

"Just leave it alone." Conrad squeezed the wheel, pushing his knuckles against his skin.

"Nah, man. I want to stop criminals when I get older. You're telling me you're going to be one of the bad guys I put in jail?"

"You're not going to catch me." He squeezed the wheel even tighter, not having to look in the mirror to know his eyes were turning blood red.

"I think I will, man. Believe me."

"Just leave it ALONE!" Conrad twisted the wheel so they went off the side of the road, stomping his foot on the break.

Chapter 38: Different

He forced his car door open, hopping out. And just as he thought,
Ethan did the same, hands balled into fists.

"Why are you doing this, Conrad?" Even though anger overcame his
entire stance, Conrad had a feeling he wasn't going to attack him. Not
yet, at least. "Just stay away from all this."

"I *can't*!" He jabbed a finger against his chest. "This is part of who I
am. Who I was meant to be. I'm not just gonna' throw it all away."

Ethan kicked at the ground, shoving his hands into his pockets. "Why? Because your dad said so? Oh, I'm sorry. Deputy?"

"You leave him out of this." Shaking his head, eyes changing into the threatening blood red color, Conrad controlled the fierce urge to tackle Ethan and throw a punch at him.

"I knew it." Ethan let out an I-can't-believe-this-mess laugh, kicking at the ground again. Conrad didn't know when the other boy became so full of himself, or why he thought it was any of his business what Conrad wanted to do with his life, but he did know he couldn't take anymore. Whirling around, speed-walking on the side of the road, the slap of shoes hitting the ground behind him suddenly overtook his attention.

"Wait, a second, civilian, put on the breaks." Against all odds, Conrad stopped, turning around to cast a glare at Timothy. The other boy struggling to catch his breath, huffing in air as if he had run a marathon. "Now, Locke understands your loyalty to these guys and everything. And hey, maybe, kind of, the thrill of committing a crime." Timothy let loose a manic chuckle, the one which made others uncomfortable. "But just know…" He shrugged. "We're worried about you, Conrad. You seem…different."

"Different." Hands going on top of his head, drifting lower so he could cover his eyes, Conrad finally flinging his hands away from his face, letting out an aggravated shout in the process. Stomping to the car, Ethan now sitting in the passenger seat with his legs hanging out the side, he went over all the things he could say. Or, all the things he wanted to say.

Hearing him coming, Ethan shot a sideways glance at him, not completely turning his head. Taking a deep breath, Conrad finally found it in himself to say after stopping, "Look, I get this isn't what I'm supposed to want in life, but this stone-I mean, it has this power-it can drain Bertram's Gift right out of him. More powerful than the shield, and those stupid bracelets. What I'm trying to say, is-I don't just want to use it for myself. I'll figure out this whole life thing later. I guess. Sometime." Once again, his hand flying up to the top of his head, fingers scratching his scalp.

Turning to look at him quizzically, mouth dropping open, Ethan putting a fist under his chin as if he was trying to solve a complex mathematical problem.

"That's the most I heard you talk, *ever.*" Mouth dropping open after he spoke, Ethan rose up from the seat he sat down on.

"A rare occurrence for our Mighty Mouse." Timothy's green eyes became wider, giving them the appearance of bright rocks. Conrad cast a glower at him, wishing he could escape the stupid name, forever.

Crossing his fingers, Ethan continued gaping at him after he spoke. "And, seriously, I want to stop Bertram as much as you, so…yeah. I'll help you find the stone. Where do we start?"

Digging around in his pocket, Conrad didn't pull his hand back out until he had the cell phone, searching for the number in his very short list of contacts. Upon finding it, he pressed the number before lifting the phone against his ear.

Chapter 39: Last One?

It took maybe four or five rings for the boss's assistant to finally answer the phone, chirping in her cheery voice, "Hello, Magnum's office. How may I help you?"

"Celia." Conrad whacked himself on the forehead, regretting letting slip he knew her first name. What was she even doing back there, anyway? "I need to talk to Magnum."

A click sounded on the other line, someone else joining their convo.

"I'm listening." The crime boss exhaled onto the phone as if he was smoking one of his cigars.

Conrad didn't bother sucking in air through his mouth to prepare himself, only speaking rapidly, "I need to see this lady hypnotist, and we need to find out where this guy went with my stone." Conrad had to steady his breathing, not the heavy gasps he thought was currently doing. Geeze, why did everything make him seem nervous all of a sudden? Because he wasn't nervous. Not in the slightest. Nope.

"In other words, you need Vanish, again? Am I right?"

"Yeah…like right now."

"Done. He'll be there before you know it." 'Click.'

"What'd he say?" asked Timothy, putting on an old street gang accent. "He gonna help us or what?"

Nodding, Conrad's phone began ringing, and he flipped it out into his hand, seeing who the name was on the screen. As soon as he pushed the button to answer, Magnum abruptly said, "We also have to know where you're at."

"We're on the side of Highway fifty-one. Off the road."

"Got it." 'Click.' He almost was surprised the man was so quick to agree about helping him, not asking any more questions like he usually did. They waited some time on the side of the road, Timothy

juggling three rocks he picked up off the dirt. Ethan sitting on his

haunches before getting up to stand beside Conrad.

"This is the last one?" Ethan's hands flew into his pocket, kicking at

the dirt, Conrad thinking all his kicking had to be a nervous habit.

Conrad brought his head up and down, mouth forming into a straight

line. But not for long.

"You'll be back at Buzzard, soon."

"Not for long, though. I'm going to see if I can pick up some people.

Want to form a strong group of fighters." He paused, moving his neck

around his shoulders. "*Man*," he spouted, throwing his hands up in

the air. "I wish you could be one of them. You and this fool, right

here." He motioned to Timothy, who made himself comfortable on

the cement, legs folded, hands on his knees.

"Hey." Timothy did a half turn on the ground. "You know Locke

has his own business to take care of."

"What is it you're going there for, again?" Conrad's eyes went to

Timothy, waiting for an answer.

"Warren wants a report on club science. Wants to see what all the fuss is about. And..." Timothy scraped his foot against the ground, staring at his shoe. "See how Gary's doing up there. Don't know how he's being treated."

Conrad watched Ethan's eyes narrow, squeezing both hands into fists. If one thing was for sure, if a kid at the school for the Gifted was giving Gary a hard time, Ethan would find him and knock him out. And if not him then the guy receiving an electric shock from Timothy would certainly ensue.

A 'Pop!' went off, putting a halt on their rants. Dusting himself off, shaking his shoes as if trying to get dirt off of them, Vanish wore a toothless smile on his face. He put his hands on his hips before saying, "Looks like you're getting another free trip."

"And you're happy about it?" Ethan cocked his head onto his shoulder, skeptical.

"Nope, but this man right here." He jabbed a finger at his chest. "Is getting a pay raise. I'm guessing all because of you, my friend." He grinned at Conrad, this time showing most of his teeth when he smiled. "Now, off to Sadie's? Yep, off to the mistress of magic, herself." He stuck out his hand. Conrad put his hand on top of his,

Timothy and Ethan doing the same. The whirl of colors, the city be-

coming a blur, Conrad's eyes snapping shut to ward off any dizziness.

Chapter 40: Sadie

Conrad shut his eyes as soon as his feet lifted into the air, only open-

ing them again as soon as they landed back on the ground, arms held

out by his sides to retain his balance. He turned his head from side to

side, observing their surroundings. If he cast his gaze to the right, he

saw part of Magnum's lair rising almost until it touched the sky, the

roof forming a square top.

He set his vision to the left, where a few small shops formed along

the sidewalk, one claiming to sell everlasting tires, while another boasted about having beautiful engagement rings. If Conrad squinted, a small store in-between the tire shop and the engagement ring place caught his eye. Walking closer so he had a better view, Sadie's Shop of Enchantment, with a long, plum colored poster displaying a new moon, and a sign sprinkled with golden confetti inviting passerby's to step inside.

"Everybody, come this way," said Vanish from out of nowhere, passing Conrad, on his way to the supposed shop of enchantment. Conrad urged himself to go forward, suddenly suspicious of the place when recalling Magnum's fondness for it. Who knew if the woman would really be willing to help them or not? Could she be going along with the crime boss's schemes and luring them into a trap? He shook his head, getting rid of the multiple doubts and worries flooding his mind.

He had to keep going, to find the stone which could take people's powers away in mere seconds. The front door, having a string of chains with bronze bells attached to them, came up in no time at all, Vanish twisting the doorknob and motioning for them to make their way inside.

More strings hanging from the ceiling, plastic plant petals attached to them, giving Conrad a trip through the jungle vibe. He swapped one of the swinging strings out of his face, smelling some kind of scent reminding him of being back in the Redwood Forest. Mixed with…he inhaled…cinnamon. Conrad gagged.

"Welcome," said a woman wearing an ocean blue silky top with matching pants, arms wide open as if she meant to embrace them. Her curly brown hair went past her shoulders, and a chain necklace jangled as she made her way toward them. She came to an abrupt stop once she was inches away from them, placing her hands on her hips.

"Now," she said, raising a hand and pointing at them with her index finger. "Conrad, Ethan, and Timothy. Is this not right?" Conrad fidgeted in his stance, goosebumps traveling up his arms, the air seeming to swirl around him.

"Oh, come on, My Darlings." She grinned, bringing her hands together. "I was told your names earlier. No need to be afraid." She pointed to a round table with a stack of cards on it, motioning for them to sit. Conrad glanced at the cards, which were all flipped over, hiding what was underneath. The only thing he could see were pictures of bright globes on the front, what Conrad guessed to be stars.

"I'll take my leave." Vanish tipped his hat, backing away, before leaving them in a strange place Conrad would rather be out of.

"Now," began Sadie, placing her hands on the table, fingers pointing at each other. "One of you needs to find something lost, stolen from you." Her eyes wondered around the table, stopping when they fell on Conrad. He shifted, shoulders going downwards, wishing all the attention wasn't on him. "Ah, I see. Tell me, Conrad, a stone was taken from you?"

"The Hidden Stone," He replied, nodding, crossing his fingers under the table.

"And your main goal is to find it, yes? Actually, you had many objectives this year, and this is your last one." Placing a hand on her forehead, Sadie tilting her head downward, she started knocking on the table with a hand curled up into a fist. He had to resist rolling his eyes, so he instead shared an irritated look with Ethan and Timothy.

He had to remember; she only used her Gift to see things. Everything else was an act she put on for paying customers. So why she was putting on a show for them, he had no idea. Unless, she wanted them to spread the word about her shop.

"I see it." She continued rubbing her forehead, letting out a gasp as if something startled her. "The man who took it…sold it in a black market, a few blocks from here." Figures. There would be a black market near Magnum's place, some hole where he could buy and sell whatever he pleased. Even if it was illegal. "Opposite from where we are. On Wayward Street. Do you know it?"

"Yep." Drumming his fingers on the table, leaning back in his seat, making himself comfortable on the hard wooden chair. Again? No cushion?

"Lady, it's been fun," spoke Timothy, standing up. "But Locke's afraid we have to-"

"Don't interrupt me!" Sadie's hand came smacking down onto the table. Dropping back into his seat, Timothy then put one hand on top of the other, turning into a kid who was afraid of disrupting the teacher.

"Young man, if you go there quickly, you can catch him before he goes off with it, keeping it for himself. Understood?" She swiped the deck of cards towards herself

"What does he look like?" Conrad's eyes met hers, finally looking away from the table.

Closing her eyes again, knocking on the table with the same fist she used last time, using the other hand to slap onto her forehead, Sadie's eyes snapped opened, staring at the space where they came in.

"A brown overcoat, black shoes, and a white top with black buttons going down the middle."

Conrad said a quick "Thanks," jumping out of his chair, not having to yell at Ethan and Timothy to hurry up. They were already out of their seats. Heading to the door, Conrad could only picture one thing. Man in black shoes. Wearing an overcoat and white top. Got it. Of all things that could happen, Vanish burst through the door Conrad was rushing to, saying with his arms spread out, "Sadie! Long time no see."

Groaning so loudly, he felt like it came from out of his whole body, he slid by Vanish and to his only way out. Out on the sidewalk, he flung the door open to the stolen car, grabbing the wheel, ready to take off and leave the other two behind. But they quickly took their seats. Ethan next to him in the front. *Finally*!

Driving in reverse, quickly looking over his shoulders, slowing down when two more cars drove past, Conrad pressed his foot on the gas as soon as the road cleared.

"Oh, man, oh, man!" Timothy shouted from the back seat, Conrad imagining him curled up in a ball. "Do we really need to go this fast?" Now that Conrad thought about it, there really wasn't any need for him to speed up the vehicle on their way to Wayward Street. He regretfully released some of the pressure he put on the gas, preferring driving at higher speeds. He may not have been his Uncle Johnny, but that didn't mean he disliked soaring down the road.

Much to Conrad's annoyance, and probably to Timothy's immense relief, they came upon a red light, forcing him to come to a stop.

"This is the right way, isn't it?" Conrad asked Ethan, his eyes still fixed on the road.

"Yeah," said Ethan, sticking his head out the window. "Wayward Street is just down here. *Gotcha'*. Conrad couldn't imagine how things could get any better. Getting his parents out of the Disappearing Hole, managing to snag Ethan and Timothy, meeting up with his number one driving teacher, and basically having the stone in his

hands. He erased any bad thoughts of how everything could mess up,

putting a damper on everything he wanted to accomplish.

Chapter 41: The Fair

A sign for Wayward Street popped up ahead of him, the letters

printed a strawberry red sign, catching to the eyed, and he guessed

pleasing to look at. To any snot nosed kids who thought they were go-

ing to an amusement park.

To his utter annoyance, a county fair, vendors selling popsicles or

lunches behind booths, a band playing instruments on a makeshift

stage, and a crowd laughing and chatting with their acquaintances.

"Why!?" He smacked a hand against the wheel, making the car's horn honk.

"Woah, man." Ethan held his hands up. "You *want* to get noticed out here? If you get seen by the cops then finding the stone will be the least of your problems." Conrad had to admit, what his brother said was alarmingly true, the scary feeling of being watched creeping up on him.

Like a sight for sore eyes, an open space by the curb invited him in. Though it may as well have been a creep behind a cheery clown's mask sine he had to park between two cars. Conrad made sure to hop out the moment after he parked, sure he wore an ultra-serious look on his face. Brows narrowed, frowning, gritting his teeth. Yeah, he needed to lighten up. He didn't want to scare any of the little kids, have them go crying to their mommies because the guy with hands balled into fists scared them.

"Look around for this guy," instructed Conrad, nearly speed-walking to the fair. "He's around here somewhere." He glanced behind himself, staring at Timothy who'd stopped walking, as still as a statue, head tilted downwards.

He slowly made his way towards him, thinking the boy resembled someone listening to a far off call.

"You okay?" Conrad hesitantly asked, turning his head to look at Ethan, but not finding him anywhere.

Timothy inhaled, sniffing a chunk of air into his nose before releasing it back out through his mouth in a heavy sigh. "Oh, it's somewhere around here." His eyes popped open, irises directed at the stage. "The electric charge it's giving out," he inhaled again. "Is causing Locke's brain cells to go haywire."

Conrad also turned his attention to the stage, where the man who shot the first thief for it came out in a black and majestic purple robe, making it swish from side to side by his legs.

Chapter 42: Rajool's Show

He held his hands up above his head, yelling out so he could be heard over the crowd, "Ladies and gentlemen, I am the mysterious Rajool, who came all the way here from over the mountains, and you are about to witness one of my greatest tricks! Something that will baffle the mind and steal the Gift out of any one who possesses it." A couple gasps went out in the crowd, some people putting their hands over their mouths. A grin spread across Razool's demeanor, putting one hand behind his back, reaching for something in his robe.

Pulling out the stone in a flourish, twisting it in his hand, showing off every part of it, Rajool beckoned for someone to step forward from behind the curtain. A young woman with dyed red hair, white tank top hanging onto her shoulder blades, stepped onto the stage, lips tightly pressed together, and having little expression in her eyes.

"Tracy will show you part of her Gift, and I, in turn, will display the power of this rock. Observe." He set the stone on the palm of one hand, holding the back of it with another. He nodded at her to begin. Tracy clapped her hands, then clenched them together and opened them in a constant motion.

A buzzing sound overflowed the entire area, Conrad observing their surroundings to see where it came from. His vision went to the sky, seeing a big group of black dots flying closer to them. He had no doubt being stung by one would bring on would bring on a ton of pain.

Descending closer to the stage so they could be near Tracy, the bees circled around her. A woman watching the show screamed. Panicked exclamations burst out, people shoving each other, attempting to be far away from the hive. Conrad was the only one who scooted up, eyes on the prize, thinking about all the ways he'd use it to deprive Bertram of his Gifts. And the rest of K.O.R.E.

The bees floated toward the rock, abandoning Tracy, who's hands dropped by her sides. They hovered around the stone for a minute longer before rising into the air, flying back to their hive. A round of applause went through the fair, along with conversations about what they just saw, some exclaiming, "Stripped the Gift right out of her!" Or, "This can stop criminals. We won't need the vigilantes, anymore."

Studying the tent on the stage, Conrad began to wrack his mind about how he could possibly retrieve the stone without being noticed. Well, he could walk in and take it, snatch it off the desk they set it on…or something like that. The only thing to do in the cool air, evening creeping onto the fairgrounds, creating a black mask over the fairgoers, was to wait for it to end. Conrad didn't care if he had to wait all night. He refused to move a muscle.

"Do we wait 'til this is over or…" Ethan appeared out of nowhere, holding a bagel powdered with sugar on the top. A stupid bagel!

"Where is Timothy?" Conrad threw his hands up, ready to rush onto the stage, himself, if they continued to stand around.

"Right behind you, sir, Conrad." Timothy stepped up, holding a mint green stuffed bear. Conrad held himself back from snatching the bear out of Timothy's hands and stomping on it. He wanted to complete one thing. *One* thing. And these morons were walking around enjoying the fair.

"Can you still sense the stone?" He gripped his hair with one hand, the 'taptaptaptap' noise his shoe made on the ground another sign of his frustration. Timothy nodded, eyeing Ethan's bagel with envy.

"It's back in the tent, -Oh, wait a minute, now it's moving. Probably to the parking lot."

Conrad stormed his way out of the fair, seeing a sign on a wooden post with an arrow pointing to where everyone was expected to park. He ranted at himself in his head for not seeing the dumb place sooner. The place was jam packed, anyway. It's not like he wanted to drive around in circles searching for a park.

Inching his way through the packed together cars, keeping a hand on the pocket on his robe, Rajool eyed the rows of cars, searching for his own. Two more men, Conrad assuming people who worked for him, stood by his sides, the one with the floppy cowboy hat on going through his cell phone, while the other, wearing a leather jacket, squatted on his hands and knees.

Not saying anything, moving closer to the men who began counting their earnings for the day, Conrad slapped his hands together once, making one of them jump, the other two jerking their heads up.

"You have something that belongs to me." Conrad pointed to himself, using his thumb. "And I want it back. The stone. Give it to me." Looking at each other, amused smiles sprouting up their faces, the presenter of their part of the show spoke with gum in his mouth.

"The only way you're getting this stone, my boy, is if I hand it to you. Which we all know is never going to happen. You and your friends need to go back to your parents. Right now." He jabbed a finger at the fair, a cheer from the crowd exploding through the air.

"I don't think you heard me" Conrad shook his head, swiping at the ground with his shoe. "That stone belongs to me. So, give it here."

"Or, what?" Rajool rubbed his hands together, snickering. "You going to take it from me, kid? Good luck."

Conrad smacked his hands together, and when he separated them, flames popped out, reaching for the showman, clawing its way towards him.

Rajool's workers scrambled back in fear, mouth's hanging open, at a loss for what to say or do.

"How interesting," said Rajool, nodding, an amused smile starting to grow up his face. "I don't have the Gift like you, so how about we compete in a different way?"

A crazy idea sprouted in Conrad's mind, waving a banner at him with bold words screaming at him what the challenge should be.

"Hey," he began, not making any movement. "How good are you at racing your car?"

Chapter 43: Driving to the Track

Getting the cars set up, Rajool even wiping off the front window with a cloth he dug out of his pocket on his jean jacket, while Conrad, opening the trunk, checked the engine. Particles of dust flew into the air, and he hastily wiped the the machine with the sleeve of his shirt.

"Alright," Rajool announced, lifting his hands up, giving a loud clap. "We will go out of the city, to the dessert East of here. I hope you're well hydrated, boy, because this place," He shook his head, thinking he was getting to Conrad. "Will suck the water right out of you." He then twisted around, motioning for his workers to follow.

"Wait, a second." Ethan jumped in front of Conrad, thrusting out an open hand. "How do you know these guys are legit? I doubt they'll give you the stone if you beat this guy."

Conrad shrugged before pushing past Ethan, making his way to his vehicle. Once he took a seat behind the steering wheel, the door opened and shut behind him. When her glanced over his shoulder at the backseat, seeing Timothy with a big, toothy grin stretching his cheeks, the door to the seat next to him opened.

Sliding inside, putting on his seatbelt, Ethan immediately saying afterwards, "I better make it to my sixteenth birthday."

"You might not." Conrad didn't bother grumbling his words, Ethan throwing him a disgruntled look. One turn of the key, one step on the gas pedal was all it took for them to race off behind Rajool's Mustang, purple lines zipping across the side of it, the same color as the purple on his robe.

He had no trouble following the Mustang, the driver zipping in and out of lanes, not appearing to care who he cut off, or who angrily honked their horn at him. Conrad had a feeling they were trying to desert him, to make sure he never caught up. But, nope. He'd get his dang stone back even if it was the last thing he ever did.

Rajool took a turn on a highway, where there was less traffic clogging up his space, Conrad staying right behind him. Eventually, the came to the side of a dirt wasteland, not a speck of plant life sprouting from the soil, everything a sandy brown. This time, Conrad wasn't reminded of the beach.

There, amongst the splashing waters, the biting cold air prickling at his skin, he'd do nothing but take a seat, throwing on a sweater two sizes too big, and burrow his hands into the pockets. This place, however, the heat blanketing on his skin, creating goosebumps across his arms and legs, whispering how it would always be there to comfort him. Well, yeah. Comforting. Even if sweat from his head, sliding down to his cheek, was a little distracting.

Conrad drove off the road as soon as the other car did, dirt crunching underneath the wheels, the wind blowing some of the scraps onto the window.

Blowing out a puff of air, his patience diminishing, he started wondering how long their journey would take. All week? Until Friday?

Rajool's driver hit the break as soon as they appeared in the middle of nowhere, Conrad leaning his head out the window.

"We're going to the edge of this dessert, where you can see the highway." Sticking his head out the door, Rajool pointed to the road they came off of. "And after that, we'll make a right, continuing till we reach the end of the dessert, and afterwards, race back to the finish line, which is where we started. All good? Do you understand?"

Conrad honked his horn twice, hoping the man understood his way of saying 'Yes.'

"Well, Locke's had fun back here, but he's afraid it's time to leave." The sound of Timothy's pants scooting across the seat. A car door opening and closing. *Figures.* Conrad didn't know what else to do except grumble some more to himself about the dumb boy who feared fast driving. He would have continued grouching to himself, but the tiny hairs on the right side of his face rose, alerting him he was being stared at.

"You leaving, too?" Conrad kept his eyes on the steering wheel, tapping a finger against it. At first, Ethan did nothing but rub his shoes on the ground, fingers clinching the sides of his shirt.

"Nah." Waving a hand in front of his face, casting an excited look at Conrad, he slid down in his seat. "I want to experience this. Forget Timothy, man. Let's win this race. Just, uh, don't crash into anything...*Please*." A chuckle came out of Conrad's throat, unbelief at the other boy's doubts tickling his funny bone.

One of Rajool's workers came out in front of the cars, holding two flags. He shook them a little by his sides. Conrad clutched the steering wheel, heart pounding in anticipation. The man held up the flags above his head for a few seconds, before forcing them down, making them flap in the wind.

Pressing hard on the gas, flying back in his seat as the car shot forward, he listened with satisfaction as the engines let out a roar.

Chapter 44: Flying down the road

The dessert zooming past him, eyes focused on what lay in front of him, including what was behind him, which happened to be Rajool.

Okay, okay. You're winning. Stay focused. Don't let him pass you.

Flinging the wheel to the right, he made sure their car was now racing towards the end of the highway, leaving Rajool in the dust. At least, he thought the man was now far behind him. Taking Conrad by surprise, the Mustang came up behind him, twisting by his side until they were neck and neck.

He didn't know what else to do but slow down as the highway was coming to an end. He turned the wheel once he reached where the dessert broke off into the road, heading back to the starting point. Rajool wasn't going to let him get away. Flying after him, the Mustang had dirt shooting out from the back of it, the wheels spitting out waste. Conrad had to keep flying down the dessert, to keep his foot on the gas pedal. Isn't that what he always told himself? *Keep going, you have to keep going.*

The man with the flags stepped over to where they were supposed to finish, waving his hands above his head, then bringing the left one down once Conrad sped past him. Rajool came after him, scowling.

Full of the utmost relief, putting his foot on the break, they came to a complete stop. Jumping up and down, waving his hands in the air, was Timothy, shouting in joy.

Looking beside himself at a huffing Ethan, who had his hands on the seatbelt across his lap, Conrad unlocked the doors, not getting out until Ethan caught his breath again.

The slamming of a car door. Shoes stomping on the ground, Rajool looking Conrad up and down when reaching him, crossing his arms.

"No," he snapped, Conrad expecting him to stomp his feet like a two-year-old. "The stone belongs to me, now. You may have stolen it yourself, but it doesn't mean I'm giving it up."

"He won the race," Ethan snapped, moving forward. "Y'all agreed-"

"Yes, yes," grouched Rajool, "but it makes no difference. I'm not giving it back to him. You'll never see it again-" His happiness at winning the race crumpling into mold, Conrad then focused on the sore loser standing in front of him, narrowing his eyes, making black smoke rise out of the man's shirt.

A 'Pow!' burst out as flames covered Rajool's right arm, his feet lifting from the ground, his whole body floating in the air.

"Alright, you can have it!" the man cried out, obviously in a lot of pain from the searing hot fire engulfing his arm. "Just put out this blasted fire!" Ethan waved his fingers downward, placing him on the ground, both of his palms facing outward as if he dared the man to go back on his deal, again.

Rajool beckoned for one of his workers to get the stone from behind the stage, giving Conrad a terrified look. As soon as they came back out, the stone wrapped in a midnight blue cloth, he dropped it into

Conrad's outstretched hands, a glare wrinkling his forehead, eyes boiling with hatred.

"You know," he began, eyes narrowed. "You're still a good-for-nothing thief who doesn't deserve this stone."

"And you do?" countered Conrad. "Look, if we're going to talk about who really deserves this, I'm going to say-" He fell silent, studying the wrapped-up stone in his hand. He locked eyes with Rajool, again, not holding back a tiny smile from climbing up his face. "I'm not even going to bother. See ya,' Rajool." *Or maybe not.*

If he felt like it, he would've continued speaking, saying, "I found it, first. You're just mad I took it before you did." He knew the power of the stone attracted a lot of criminals who thought they could use it whenever a vigilante showed up and tried to stop their plans. He decided to get rid of the thought, focusing, instead, on his two brothers. He wasn't sure when he'd ever see them again

"I guess you know what happens next." Ethan's hands went into his pockets, giving Conrad a solemn look.

"Yeah...Buzzard Island?"

295

"Yes, indeedy," said Timothy, kicking one foot behind the other. "Locke has to get ready for this trip to the school for the Gifted. Dazzle and amaze them with our Club Science intellect."

"Yeah." Ethan ran a hand through his hair. "And I need to see how many people are willing to join me to defeat this sucker. Wouldn't hurt to ask."

Chapter 45: Conrad's Departure

Sticking a hand in his pocket, Conrad finally found the cell phone he
was looking for, having to wiggle his fingers around.

"You guys know I can't stay on Buzzard." He shook his head, kicking at the ground. "But...we'll probably see each other, again. I don't
know."

"Man, of course we'll see each other again." Ethan rolled his eyes.
"Are you kidding me?" While Timothy and Ethan continued their

conversation, he already had Vanish on the phone, the man's grouchy voice putting a hurting on Conrad's eardrum.

"Where are you, now?" Vanish grouched, and Conrad wondered if his pay raise had gone down. He quickly gave their location, Vanish appearing in no time at all, afterwards. After he dropped them off back at the island, the salt water smell plus the plant life attacking his nostrils, Conrad felt inside his pocket. He snatched up the note he wrote for Beverly then gave it to Ethan, her name scrawled in the middle in his sloppy handwriting.

"What the-" Timothy regarded the note Conrad had quickly told Ethan about, beforehand.

"See, ya.'" Conrad gave a quick one-handed wave, backing up towards Vanish. The last thing he heard while disappearing with Vanish was Timothy's loud mouth. And honestly, he was okay with that.

Epilogue

Wrists tied together with a cloth Bertram tore from a sheet out of anger, Gary sat in a room he was sure they used for medical purposes. Beds with clean sheets stretched across them, taunting him about how he wasn't allowed to move from his chair, were spread around the room, right next to each other on stands.

He moved his feet, sliding them across the shiny tiles, his black and white Converse sneakers having been snatched off, leaving him with nothing but white socks going up past his ankles.

A chill made him shiver, the air conditioner blasting out cold air in the room he couldn't remember walking into. Nothing made sense, anymore.

'Bam!' The door to the room he sat in was flung open, hitting a wall to the side of it.

Gary struggled in his seat as soon as he saw who walked in, accompanied by two security guards. Charlotte Beauregard's thin red skirt extended until it hit the tips of her silver pumps, the matching blazer she wore completely buttoned up.

She flipped her curled hair over her shoulder, not losing her tooth bearing smile.

"Hello, sweetie," she coo' d, patting him on the head. Gary tried thrusting himself forward, but the straps tied around him made moving nearly impossible.

"This will only take a few seconds, I promise. All I'm going to do is look into your eyes, and you'll feel like a whole new person." Gary ardently shook his head, only to have Charlotte jerk his chin down. He snapped his eyes closed, one of the guards she came in with grasping at his cheeks, creating a spiral of pain which forced him to open his eyes.

Charlotte saw it as the right time to widen her own round shaped eyes, and Gary's mind was suddenly overflooded with images of himself taking down a criminal, and standing tall on the back of the criminal he took down. Yes…this was right. He suddenly remembered all the fights he'd been through, all the criminals he'd defeated with his father, Bertram.

Yes, his father, Bertram Swift.

CPSIA information can be obtained
at www.ICGtesting.com
Printed in the USA
LVHW021523050121
675633LV00012B/330